Walking on Gold

This is an Electrik Inc book.

Electrik Inc is a collective combining great writing for children and young adults, sharp editing and professional independent publishing (ebooks and print on demand). With more than fifty years' industry experience between them – plus four MAs in Writing for Young People from Bath Spa University – the founders of Electrik Inc have one objective: to make each book the best it can be.

http://electrikinc.wordpress.com

Walking on Gold

Janine Amos

DANCING HARE

Published by Dancing Hare

ISBN: 978-0-9929593-0-2

To my family

One

I get home from school and the telly's gone. In its place is a pile of boxes.

I know what this means.

A big red *No* bubbles up from my insides. "You promised!" I shout. "You promised we'd never move again!"

Mum's in the kitchen, banging about, shoving things into black bin liners. She swings round towards me. Her hair's tied back in a scrunchie and her face looks all hot and pink.

"It's the last time, Effie," she says. "Honest, Fee."

Fee is what she always calls me when she wants something.

We always get what she wants. This time I want something. I want to stay living in this flat, go to this school. I want to have friends round for tea. I want to have sleepovers. I want to be like normal people. I don't want to always be the new girl.

"I'm not going," I tell her. "We've only lived here three weeks!"

I run to my bedroom, slam the door and throw myself on my bed. Mum never keeps her promises. I push my face deep into the duvet and feel hot tears squeeze out the corners of my eyes. I never cry. Inside I'm on fire, like I'm about to explode.

Much later, Mum opens my door and stands in the doorway. I keep my head turned away but she just comes in and sits down next to me.

"Come on, come and help me pack." Her voice is all bright and shiny. "It's the last time, I promise."

"La-la-la," I go inside my head.

She carries on. "We're going back to my island – where I was born. We'll see Uncle Jim. It'll be great. We'll have all summer there and you can start your new school in September. We'll live there forever – no moving, ever again."

I turn round to face her. "How long have you known?" I ask.

"Not long." Mum looks away. "I wanted to get it sorted before I said anything."

I've heard it all before, six times before. Six new schools and six times being the new girl. Being different, all over again.

"I'm not going," I shout. I grab my pillow and throw it down on the floor. I kick my duvet off, too. I want to chuck everything round my room. "I'm not going to your stupid island!"

Two days later we're off.

Two

The boat is hot and crammed with people. Everything's really loud – two women shouting at their little kids, a baby crying, and a big man in a stripy tee shirt laughing his head off. Mum and me are squashed up on some hard metal seats next to a spotty boy with an iPod blaring out. The engine shakes and throbs and my mouth fills with hot liquid.

"Quick! Up on deck!" Mum grabs my arm and pushes me towards some steps. We have to climb over the piles of bags and boxes that stick out all over the floor.

On the deck I get a whiff of suntan lotion, egg sandwich and Mum's new perfume. I throw up over the side of the boat.

Afterwards I'm cold and shivery, with a horrible taste in my mouth, so Mum gives me a bottle of water and some tissues from her bag.

Sitting on the floor with a wet tissue over my eyes, I start to feel better. It's OK up here, the air is cool even though it's summer, and the wind tugs my hair. Soon I ball up the tissue and look around for Mum.

She's standing at the railings, gazing out to sea. Suddenly she makes a weird noise, like a yelp.

"There it is!" she shouts, leaning over the side of the boat. "There's the island!"

I scramble up and run to look where she's pointing. In the far, misty distance is a tiny hump of land poking out of the grey waves.

"Our new home," she says.

I stare and stare until my eyes water.

On the quay, a tall skinny man walks up to us. He's got a shaved head and a small earring in one ear.

"Jim!" says Mum. She sounds all snuffly, like

she's got a cold, and I know she's going to cry.

"Welcome home, Penny," he says.

Uncle Jim, Mum's brother. He's all the family we've got in the whole world. Except for Raine, but we're not counting her.

Jim puts his arms round Mum and gives her a great big hug. Who knows how long it's going on for, so I shuffle my feet and shift my rucksack onto the other shoulder.

He looks at me then.

"And hello to you, Effie. Welcome to our island." His voice is soft with a funny roll to it, like a growl. He gets my hand and half-shakes, half-squeezes it, pulling me a bit towards him. His baggy blue tee shirt smells of washing powder. Around his neck is a string of leather with three brown beads.

Mum's talking really fast. "It's brilliant to see you. After all this time! I can't believe we're really here. We must get our bags and …"

Her face is bright red and she's got tears running down her cheeks – happy tears –though it's weird to see her cry in front of Jim. I try to give her the tissues back but she's too busy talking and doesn't see me, so I blow my own nose instead.

Jim picks up the big bags we've got with us and slings them across his shoulders.

We follow him to the place where all the baggage is being unloaded from the boat. Our two rucksacks with the bright yellow stickers are easy to see, squashed between two crates of vegetables. Jim finds a massive metal trolley, like a cage on wheels, and we heave the bags into it. Then he pushes it across the quay, away from the crowds, to a little blue truck.

"Hop in," he tells us. "Rosa's making something to eat, so we'll go to our place first. Afterwards I'll take you up to the house and show you round."

The truck's only got two seats, and I have to climb into the open back part with the bags. There's an old tyre to sit on, with a tatty yellow blanket thrown on top.

Jim gets going and I bounce along, looking out at the town. Everything's tiny – the houses are small and jumbled up together, a bit like a miniature world. It's still the afternoon but the streets around here are empty and I can't see one supermarket or shopping mall. Where is everyone?

Behind the streets I can see trees and high green hills, stretching up and up into the sky.

I can't believe we'll be living here for good.

Once we get away from the harbour, the roads are dusty with no cars. The houses look all closed-up as if they're asleep. It's really quiet.

We turn up a street with a launderette on the corner. Jim stops the truck and lets down the back for me to get out.

"Come and meet Rosa," he says, jiggling his keys about in his hand.

He opens a yellow front door, and Mum and me follow him through a dark hallway. There's another door with a glass panel just in front of us. Jim pushes it with his shoulder and it swings back.

It smells like Christmas inside.

The tiny room is crammed with furniture but it's full of light, with white curtains flapping at an open window. A woman with long black hair comes towards us.

"Penny! Effie! Hello!" she calls. Under her arm she's got a fat baby who stares at me with round brown eyes. It sticks its fist in its mouth and screams.

"Shh, Bee." Rosa jogs the baby up and down, talking at the same time. Her words come tumbling out: "There, there, it's all right. Bee – this is your Aunty Penny and your cousin Effie. Jim – get the food, it's all ready. Now, sit yourselves down, you're tired and hungry; it's a very late lunch."

We sit round the wooden table covered with food – huge chunks of bread and a massive green salad. Jim gets a red dish out of the oven and takes off the lid. It's a meaty stew and my stomach leaps. I'm starving.

We pile up our plates and I'm stuffing my mouth full of bread and gravy when the door opens. In walks a boy with straight black hair like Rosa's, and the same tanned skin. He looks a bit older than me – nearly teenage. Moving soft and quick like a cat, he pulls off his sweatshirt and throws it on a chair.

Rosa stands up, still holding the baby. "Luke, I asked you not to be late. Penny and Effie are here."

She sounds like she's telling him off but she's smiling, too.

The boy smiles back, a big, wide smile exactly like Rosa's. "Hi, everyone," he says, slipping into the seat across from me.

"This is Rosa's son, Luke," Jim tells me. "He helps out on the fishing boats, down at the quay."

I watch Luke. He tears the bread and dips it into the stew like he hasn't had anything for weeks. He sees me looking.

"Starving. Been getting in the catch." He gulps between mouthfuls.

I don't know what he means.

It's a noisy meal. Mum keeps saying to Jim, "Remember when …?" and they laugh together and go on about something that happened years ago. Rosa rocks the baby, curled in her lap, falling asleep with its hand buried in her hair.

"Lantern Rock. Oh, I love that place," says Mum, with a dreamy look in her eyes, "and Bishops Sound …"

And off they go, everyone talking about places I've never been, with weird-sounding names: Petrel Point, Casey's Cove, Dazeyman's Reef.

Mum's eyes are shining. "There's so much for me to paint here. I can't wait to catch a sunrise over Hetty's Bay," she says.

I sit only half-listening, picking at the breadcrumbs left on my plate. Nothing makes sense – all these people with their funny voices, talking about stuff I've never heard of. I can't believe Mum wants us to stay here. There's got to be a way for us to go back to the mainland. Somehow.

Luke wipes his mouth with the back of his hand and talks to Jim across the table. "More divers came in – from America, this time. They're going off that big wreck, out near Lantern Rock."

"Be careful, Luke," says Rosa. "You know I don't like you hanging around with strangers."

"They're OK, Mum." Luke looks at me. "We're always getting treasure hunters here," he boasts, "diving for gold and stuff. There's thousands of gold coins out there somewhere."

"I bet you didn't know you were coming to a real treasure island, did you Effie?" Jim says.

Is he joking? I hope not 'cos it's the best thing I've heard all day.

Three

When the food's all gone, Luke gets up and goes to the window, looking out. He flicks the window latch backwards and forwards with his finger *ping, ping, ping*.

Rosa stops talking to Mum and Jim. "Luke, why don't you take Effie over to the house? We'll catch you up."

"Let's go," says Luke, moving towards the door and grabbing an apple from the fruit bowl as he goes.

Halfway down the hallway he stops and turns round. I can smell his breath, warm and fruity from the apple.

"Wait 'til you see it. You'll be living in a real haunted house. How lucky is that."

"What?" It's too dark to see if he's teasing.

"Whoo-ooh! Scared of ghosts, are you?" He flaps his arms about and pushes open the front door.

He's just the same as the boys who hang round the flats at home. Stupid.

"I'm not scared of anything," I say.

Luke runs across the road and dodges down an alley opposite, and I follow him. The ground's dusty with sand, a thin layer of dirty yellow. Empty crisp packets and an old carrier bag bounce along next to us in the wind. It doesn't look very scary so far.

At the end of the alley the houses stop. In front of us is a steep, grassy hill with a zigzag path going up. Luke rushes towards it.

The wind rips through my hair and the air is cold and salty, the same as on the boat.

"Is it far?" I shout, but my words disappear in the wind and my hair flies into my mouth, like fine salty string.

At the top of the hill there's a massive old house with trees and bushes all around. Luke's leaning against a curly iron gate, waiting for me.

"This is it," he says. "Crow House."

I look past him to the crumbling stone building, standing all on its own. It's like a huge, sleeping face, with a chimney each end for ears and big dark windows upstairs for eyes. Why's Mum brought me here? Why can't we live somewhere ordinary? A normal house in a normal street. I either get to live in stinky, mean tower blocks or a spooky place like this.

But I don't say a word.

"It's great." Luke slips in through the gate and pushes a way through all the green stuff, round to the back.

We stand in the garden. It's wild, though I can see that the grass was once an old-fashioned lawn. Around the edges, huge bushes with shiny leaves and big pink flowers droop onto the grass.

The wind makes the tall trees rattle. "Told you – ghosts and demons," says Luke, opening his eyes wide.

A skinny grey cat dashes out of the trees and across the grass in front of me.

"Demon Number One," he whispers.

We follow the cat round the side of the

house. Here the trees bend right over, 'til the tips of their branches touch the rough, grey stone. Scraggy plants sprout out the wall like whiskers.

"Why's it empty? Where have the people gone?"

"I said: it's haunted …" Luke watches my face, and grins. "Nah – it's just falling down, that's all."

"I can't believe Mum wants to live here."

"No money, that's why. Raine owns it and she's letting your mum rent it dead cheap, as a favour. Jim said. Your mum's got no job and no money, and this is all she can afford."

I turn on him. "Shut up! You think you know everything! My mum will be famous one day: a famous artist. Then you'll be sorry!"

I run round to the front of the house, and my head's full of a hot, angry buzzing.

Mum, Jim and Rosa are coming up the hill, little dots bobbing against the wide greenness. I sit down to wait for them, grabbing handfuls of the spiky grass. I hate Luke saying that about Mum. She doesn't need a job, she sells her paintings. Sometimes she does.

Rosa is first up the hill, in her bright red dress

with yellow flowers. Mum and Jim are walking together, with baby Bee on Jim's back in a kind of rucksack.

Rosa sinks down next to me, flattening herself into the grass a bit like a giant butterfly. I can smell her scent, sweet and spicy, mixed with smells from her cooking.

We don't say anything for ages. I tug more grass and let it swirl away in the wind.

At last Rosa speaks. "You're angry. You've been fighting with Luke." She reaches out to touch my face and her hand smells of onions. Up close, I can see that Rosa has spots of gravy on her dress and little specks of it clinging to her hair. Around her neck she's got a bead necklace, like Jim's.

Mum and Jim get to the top of the hill and walk past us.

"You'll soon be friends again, you'll be friends forever." Rosa says it softly, like a charm.

I kind of snuggle down and look *into* the grass. It's made up of different things, not like the grass in parks. There's tall, tufty stuff and little green plants with frilly edges and it's all different sorts of green. There's bugs in here

– little hoppers almost too quick to see – and slow-moving spiders creeping and crawling. I don't mind them, it's their home and I'm the giant stranger.

Then Mum's calling from inside the house, "Come on! The door's open."

I get up and go through the gate, over the doorstep, and into a long hallway with rooms on both sides. I can hear Luke thumping about upstairs. Everywhere is cold and bare and echoey. In the kitchen I find Mum and Jim leaning against the sink, looking out into the tangly back garden.

"Yes, it's a jungle. But we'll all help," Jim is saying. "I'll get a lawnmower up here and cut the grass. It's Luke's school holidays; he can give me a hand."

"We'll manage," says Mum. "We always do, don't we, Effie?"

I look around me. The tap goes *drip-drip-drip*. The window over the sink is broken and part of it is covered with dirty brown board. There's a mouldy smell. I hate it all.

"I cleaned it up as much as I could – we only got the keys on Friday," Rosa says, coming in and pointing to the shelves. "There are two saucepans and a frying pan. Jim's bought a new kettle …"

Jim jigs baby Bee up and down on his back. He isn't smiling. "There's a lot to do, Pen," he says to Mum. "But you were lucky to get it. Houses on the island are like gold dust."

Above us, Luke's walking about, making the floorboards groan.

"Go and find your bedroom, Effie," Mum says. "You like to do that."

I walk out of the kitchen and up the stairs towards the footsteps. They stop and then Luke's peering down at me.

"Found the ghost yet?" He flashes a smile.

"What's upstairs?" I ask.

"Empty rooms, with millions of dead flies and cobwebs. I bet you'll scream: *I'm not sleeping here!*" He says it in a high, stupid voice.

I ignore him and march on up the creaky stairs, past a big window, to a landing. The walls are brown and stained. This place is just as bad as Ellsmere Flats. Worse.

The first bedroom is huge with bare floorboards and a big bed in the middle. Through the windows, I can see the massive, grey sky above the wide, flat sea. Spiders' webs hang from the corners of the windows, with dead flies trapped in them. There's dead flies on the windowsill too, and one dried-up brown spider.

Next door is another room, a bit smaller. A window is cracked and has black tape right across it. Everything's dusty and grey and sad-looking. Two other rooms are locked.

Luke comes in with the cat in his arms. "Look who I've caught – your ghost-cat."

The cat waves the tip of its tail dangerously. It struggles and claws at Luke's bare skin.

"OW!" he shouts, dropping it to the floor. It races out of the room and I hear it pelt down the stairs.

I burst out laughing. "Serves you right."

Jim goes off to get the bags. Our duvets and stuff are coming on another boat so Rosa helps us sort out sheets and blankets. We put some on Mum's bed and some in the small room for me.

It's late when everyone leaves. I go back upstairs and Mum's sitting on the windowsill, which is like a seat, right on top of all the dead flies. She's got a bottle of red wine open next to her and a big glassful in her hand.

"It'll be OK living here," she says, looking out through the window. She's put the lamp on next to the bed and her hair shines all soft and silvery. "It'll look different in the morning, when the sun's out. You can go on the beach and play with Luke and …"

"Play? I'm not a little kid! It's horrible here. It's boring and it stinks." She never understands. I squeeze my hands hard into fists.

Mum sighs. "You'll have to make the best of it."

She's got something hanging round her neck on a golden chain. It's a brown bead, just like Jim's and Rosa's.

"What's that?" I snap at her. But I get nearer to have a proper look.

"It's my sea-bead," she says, slow and sleepy. "All the Islanders have one; pirate treasure lost in a shipwreck hundreds of years ago." She puts her hand to her neck and touches the bead. "Jim's been taking care of it for me, all these years."

I stand looking at Mum and the bottle of

wine, and suddenly I'm really tired.

"I'm going to bed," I say.

I don't bother to clean my teeth. Next door, in the little bedroom, I lie down and pull up the covers. The rough blanket smells like a charity shop and it makes my nose itch. This is the worst place we've ever been.

The wind moans a lonely old song.

Four

I wake up with the sun bright in my face.

Kicking off the smelly blanket, I scramble to the window. Outside it's like a whole new world: a light blue sky, a dark blue sea and white waves dazzling and dancing.

I pull on my clothes and tiptoe past Mum's room and down the stairs. When I yank open the front door, a rush of air comes at me, all cold and clean and sharp. The sea is rolling and sighing *whoosh-aaah, whoosh-aaah*. Two white birds scream and dip right over my head, then roll and tumble away in the big, big sky.

A gust of wind blows, making my arms prickle with goosebumps. I zip up my fleece –

and the cat from yesterday slips in past my legs like a thin grey shadow.

I follow him into the kitchen. *Me-ow*, he goes, *me-ow*. I expect he's hungry but there's no food here for cats, just some bread in a packet and a lump of cheese in the fridge, where Rosa put it. I get some of the food and go over to the back door to let the sunshine in. Shadow the cat sticks to my legs like glue. We sit on the step in the sun and I feed him little pieces of cheese. One for him, one for me.

He's all stretched out, having a rest after breakfast, when his ears twitch. Someone's coming. Shadow gets to his feet and disappears into the garden.

"Hello! Anyone there?" It's Rosa. She comes round the side of the house, a flash of red from her flowery dress, with Bee in a buggy. Bee's fat little arms are reaching out – reaching for me – and she's making little squealing sounds: "Eh, Eh!" like she's trying my name. I hold out my hand and she grabs one finger really tight.

"Someone's pleased to see you," Rosa says. "We're going to the beach – do you want to come?"

I fetch my trainers and I'm ready.

"Where's your mum?" Rosa asks. "We'd better let her know where you're going."

I say that Mum's asleep and we mustn't disturb her. Rosa gets a worried little line between her eyes. She goes on that we have to let Mum know. And that we must get the phone connected.

All I want to do is get on the beach.

In the end, we write a note and leave it on the kitchen table. I know Mum won't come down to read it for hours but it makes Rosa happy. And off we go along the zigzag path, down the green hillside – and there's the sea stretched out, wide and blue and rolling.

Rosa keeps on walking, past the beach, which is right there in front of us.

"We're going to a different beach – to hunt for treasure," she tells me.

"What do you mean?"

"Wait and see." She pushes the buggy really fast, sending Bee bouncing up and down.

We follow another grassy path up and away from the town. The air is cold, and it smells different, a bit like the city farm mixed with the seaside. Tall pink flowers bend right over in the wind. Great gusts of it blow in my eyes. And it's loud too, roaring and howling along with the sea. I open my mouth wide and drink in a cold, salty nothing. The wind lifts up Rosa's hair and throws it back from her face and her dress flaps about her like a fluttery red flag. I stick out my arms and stand firm as my fleece is tugged and pulled and shaken. It's brilliant!

Bee loves it too. "Eeeeh!" she squeals. "Eeeeh!" like the wind's a big, exciting monster and we're doing battle with it – and winning. Her hood's pulled up and it's filled with wind, puffed up around her head in a fat blue halo.

The path's almost disappeared now. Instead, the ground is covered with short purple plants – heather, Rosa says it is – springy and bouncy under our feet, and yellow bushes called gorse. We're going down again, down to the beach.

The wind's gone – my ears are ringing from the quiet – and, suddenly, it's warm.

Rosa stops and lifts Bee out of the buggy and onto her hip. She gets a bag from the drawer part under the seat, folds up the buggy and lays it on the ground.

"Can you carry this for us, please?" she asks, holding out the bag to me.

Struggling and slipping, we scramble over rocks onto the yellow sand. It stretches in a huge curve with the moving sea in the middle. There's little pools of water and humps of brown seaweed everywhere.

Far away, over the other side, I can see just three other people.

"Nice and quiet. Too tucked away for tourists," Rosa says. She kicks off her sandals, wobbling on one leg with Bee in her arms, and sinks down onto the sand.

I want to know about the treasure.

"There is treasure here, if you dig for it," Rosa tells me. "This is where the beads come from. There aren't so many left these days but you might be lucky."

"What about treasure chests? Gold coins and jewels and stuff?" I ask her. "Like Luke was talking about yesterday."

Rosa laughs. "Maybe. Though I think you have to dive for that. But if you find a bead, we'll make you a necklace like mine."

I start digging in the cold, wet sand.

I move a bit away from Rosa, because Bee's shuffling round on her bottom and messing up my digging holes. I'm next to a rock pool, heaving up stones, sending quick little fishy things darting about in the water. My digging makes it go a cloudy brown and it's hard to see so I scoop about in the freezing cold water, bringing out handfuls of grit. I grab hold of big shells and use them as diggers. I find a flat rock and pile up the sand in heaps, sorting through it, working out a system: dig, scoop, pile, sort. Over and over again.

Rosa comes up next to me, holding Bee. "Look at you, you're wet," she says.

I am. My trainers are soaking and my bum's got a wet patch from dipping down in the water.

"Come and have a sandwich," she says.

She's got a picnic. I leave the digging and we sit further up the beach on the dry sand, eating cheese sandwiches and ham. There's crisps and apples too.

"Nearly time to head home," says Rosa.

"But I haven't found a bead!"

Suddenly I want one so much it's like an ache inside.

"There'll be plenty of other times," she says, packing up her bag. "You live here now, don't forget."

All the way back up the beach I'm looking for beads. I know what Rosa says is right, but I can't stop looking down, hoping to see one lying there, next to a shell or a stone. I kick through the sand with my trainers, scuffing it up, hunting. My eyes are sore with looking.

Rosa knows. "You're just as likely to find beads in the fields these days," she tells me, "right near Crow House."

We get back to Crow House and go up to see Mum. She's sitting on her bed with her sketchbook on her lap and she's gazing out across the sea.

"I know about Beady Bay," I tell her. "We've been there – and we had a picnic – and I've been digging for hours, but I haven't found one single bead."

"Yet," says Rosa, and we laugh.

There's a noise from downstairs. Someone's calling:

"Hello! Shall I come up?"

Rosa stops and looks across at Mum.

Mum whispers one word: "Raine", and I

know my grandmother is down there.

The staircase creaks – she's on her way up.

I've got shivers all over and my heart's banging away in my chest. And before I'm ready, Mum's bedroom door opens and here she is, right in front of me – Raine.

Mum's enemy.

Thin and tall and mean-looking, Raine's got black trousers on and a white shirt, like a man's. Her white, white hair is pulled back tight from her face, and her eyes are like ice. There's two rows of bright shiny beads hanging round her neck.

"You came," she says, staring right at me.

Bee gives a long, high wail.

Raine looks over at Mum. "I knew you'd come back one day."

"Yes," says Mum in the quietest mouse-voice ever.

There's a big, long silence and I think about all the horrible things Mum's told me about Raine: how she was such a mean, strict parent with loads of rules and punishments. I stand in the dusty room and glare at her 'til I think I'll burst.

Mum just sits there, looking down at her

sketchbook. Rosa's fussing with Bee.

"Well, are you settling in?" Raine asks, her ice-eyes fixed on Mum.

Mum nods.

"And how about you, Effie? How do you like it here?" Raine says.

I look round me at the spiders' webs and the dirty window and the walls black with damp. I'm saying nothing.

"Don't turn your nose up, young lady."

"What? Like yours?" I only think it but I know I'm scowling hard.

Then I run.

I hate it: this dark, grey house and the horrible, mean grandmother. Down the stairs I go, jumping two at a time. I yank open the front door and run out into the fresh air, ramming my feet down into the grass. The wind catches my hair and flings it back, hard, in my face.

Mad as anything, I race past the front of Crow House, along the cliffs, away from the town. The sea below me is dark and wild, with crazy foaming waves. It roars and crashes – in – against the rocks and hisses – out – over the pebbles, a great angry beast of a sea breathing its huge watery breaths.

My feet pound on the cliff path, sending little chips of stone bouncing down, down – smash! – onto the beach. I'm running so hard, my chest's burning.

I head away from the sea and the path disappears. The grass is short and springy, with ferns and lumps of rock. Huge, round boulders stand in groups, like they're giants having a chat. Giants turned to stone. The noise of the waves is only a whisper here.

My breathing is a sharp pain. I flop down on the grass next to a rock shaped like a witch, taking great gulps of air, drowning on land.

I sit for a long time, leaning against the rock, panting and puffing, just breathing. Prickly yellow gorse is all around and the air smells of coconuts. Great white birds zoom above me, filling the air with their shrieks.

I close my eyes and see Raine, standing in the bedroom, with those shiny beads round her neck. I dig my fingers into the ground but it's not sand this time, it's grass and earth, soft and cold.

I reach down and down until I feel something sharp. I close my fingers around it and pull it out, covered with soil and bits of pebble.

It's round and flat – a medal, or something. It sits in my hand, heavy with earth. I rub it against my jeans, getting the dirt off. Fixed on the back there's a long metal pin; it must be a badge or a brooch. I can make out a carving – a bird's head. The beak is hooked, like an eagle's, and one fierce eye glares up at me.

The whole thing winks in the sunlight.

Gold.

A voice calls my name, Luke's voice. My heart is banging in my chest. I slip the brooch in my pocket, stand up and kick the soil back into the hole. I stamp the grass down and hurry to the path.

Luke's running towards me. When he sees me, he stops. "Hey, what's going on?" he shouts.

I'm bursting with excitement but I keep my mouth tight shut.

"Raine's gone now," he says. "They sent me to get you, in case you fall off the cliff or something."

I still don't answer him.

Luke digs his hands deep in the pockets of his jeans. "It's OK here, y'know," he says. "It's not like being in a city but," he pokes about in the grass with the toe of his trainer, "it's great for swimming, and –"

"Luke – is there really treasure? Here on this island?"

"What?" He looks up at me and his eyes go sparkly. "Yeah. We get divers from all over, searching for wrecks –"

"On the land, I mean – did people bury treasure – in chests?"

"I dunno if that's just made-up –"

I don't wait for him to finish, I'm thinking out loud: "Rosa said that you can find those beads in the sea and on land – there could be treasure anywhere," I say. "Right under our feet."

Luke laughs. "Yeah, we could be walking on gold!"

I look down at the bouncy, green grass.

There is treasure buried here, all right, and I know exactly where it is.

Luke has to get home for tea so we run back together.

As we go, he points out different places. "Where we are now is Gull Head, and the beach below us is Hell's Mouth. Over there, that's Little Cove – it's great for bodyboarding at high tide. And that one's Devil's Spout. The waves there are the best on the island."

I run along the path with him, stopping to peer over the edge at the sea beating against the rocks. It's a dark greeny-blue.

"Get back!" Luke warns, as some stones break off and tumble down to the beach below. "These cliffs look strong but the edges crumble – then splat. No more Effie."

When we get to Crow House, Luke carries on down the hill.

"See you!" he calls.

"See you!" I turn in the gate and race round the back, checking that the brooch is still in my pocket.

I'm filthy. I kick off my trainers and run upstairs. I close the bathroom door softly behind me, careful not to disturb Mum, and turn the big key in the lock. Safe, I turn on both bath taps, take out my muddy treasure and lay it gently in the bath. The mud swirls about in the water, making it a cloudy yellow.

I lift the brooch from the bottom of the bath and rub away all the dirt with my flannel. Peering through the steam, I can see all the tiny lines of the bird's feathers. Who made it? Who was it for?

And how much other stuff is buried with it under that rock?

Tomorrow I'll find out.

Five

Next morning, the sky's misty-white. The first thing I do is reach under my pillow and pull out the golden brooch. There's still quite a lot of dirt stuck in the carved bits; I scrape it with my nail, making the bird stand out clearer and fiercer than ever.

I slide the brooch back safe again, right inside the pillowcase so it can't fall out, then I roll out of bed and pull on my clothes. Along the hall, I peep into Mum's room. It's smelly in there, sickly sweet, because she took some wine to bed; I can see the empty glass on the floor. She's sleeping deep with her hair all ragged on her pillow.

Downstairs, I push open the back door and go into the bushy garden, drippy-wet leaves next to my skin. Everything smells new and scenty outside, with earth and flowers mixed together. The sea's rolling and sighing like always.

I'm puffing big time when I get to Gull Head. There's no one about – except the gulls, of course. There's more of them today – huge white and grey birds with bright yellow beaks, whizzing through the air just above me. I run past them, across the springy grass towards the rocks. The wind whips around me, tugging and pulling. I see the gulls' chicks, fat and speckled, sitting on the rocks. Suddenly, the parent gulls are dive-bombing me, swooping and screaming: *Yah-yah-yah.* One comes straight for me with evil yellow eyes and an angry spot each side of its sharp beak. *Yaa-hah-haah* it laughs, swerving past my head, taking the air with it: *whap!*

I cover my head with my arms and rush across the grass, peering out through a gap in my arms in search of my digging place. Everywhere looks the same: the short grass with heather mixed in, the giant boulders. I run zigzag, tripping up on a tangly root. What if I never find the place again?

There it is – a big old rock shaped like a witch with two smaller ones next to it. I fall down on my knees and start scuffing away, digging up the earth like a dog.

I dig for hours and hours. Old bits of root, stones and shell come up – nothing shiny, though. I dig deeper, pushing both hands in up to my wrists. The hole's getting wider – but I come up against hard, flat rock, running all across the bottom of my hole. I wish I'd got a spade or something; my hands are getting sore and my fingernails are black with dirt.

Then the rock wobbles a bit, just a tiny bit, but I'm sure I felt it move. Yeah. In my head there's a picture of a big wooden chest, filled with golden coins. My arms are so tired, and it's really hot. I push and kick the rock with my feet, to give my arms a rest.

It won't come. I feel tears start behind my eyes, but I blink them away. I'm starving hungry, it must be nearly lunchtime, and I've not found a thing. There's more gold down there, I know it. I just need a proper spade or something, to get down under the rock. I'll have to go home for now – but I'm not giving up. Never.

Like before, I cover up my digging. It's harder to push back the heather this time, and I'm in a hurry, so it looks a bit messy. No one comes up here anyway, I hope.

As I go back across the grass, the gulls start up again but I don't mind them, and I follow the path back to Crow House.

I'm just walking up the last stretch, near the wood, when there's voices in the trees. Boys' voices. There's a laugh, and I know one of them is Luke.

"Shh!" goes someone.

I come off the path and creep a bit nearer to listen, hiding myself in the bushes.

"Tonight then, and don't forget the torch," says one of them.

"Are you in – or not?" says another boy.

"Yeah. See you later!"

I peep out and here's Luke's cat-smile, right next to my face.

"Effie!"

I dodge back in the bushes but it's too late. He's cut through the trees ahead of me.

"Are you SPYING on me?"

I keep my mouth shut tight.

The other boys crowd in too, and they're all talking at once:

"Is this your cousin?"

"Sort of," says Luke.

"What's she doing? Following us?"

"What did she hear?"

I make my eyes go big and wide. Luke looks at me hard. I still don't say a thing. We stand there, eyeballing each other.

In the end he gives up. "Just you watch out," he says.

I nod at him and squeeze past, back towards the path.

Luke's got a secret too.

Six

It's chips for tea. Mum and me have huge piles of them with loads of sauce and vinegar. I love vinegar, I put on so much that the bottom ones go brown and soggy. Sometimes Mum calls me the Vinegar Queen. Not today.

"That stinks," she says, moving up the settee, away from me.

I just grin and wave a soggy chip at her. We've got the TV going and she's flicking through the channels.

"Oh, let's watch this," she says, finding a film just about to start. "The oldies are always the best."

I stop eating, a chip halfway to my mouth.

"Aren't we going down to Rosa's?"

"Let's give them an evening to themselves," she says, putting her empty plate down on the floor. "We don't want to wear out our welcome." And she laughs, to show it's a joke, but in a way that means it might be true.

Typical. Why tonight? Tonight I need to find out where Luke's going, which means I have to get round his house before he goes.

So I settle down for a wait.

The film's quite good really. There's a sad part in the middle, which makes Mum cry a bit, and a happy end part. That makes her cry too.

She gets the wine out then, and I know it won't be long before she has a doze.

I watch part of the next show, then it's the News. I think about switching channels but the remote's right near Mum's hand, and she's nodding off nicely. Mustn't leave it too long because it's feeling really late. My eyes are aching and my body is too, from all that digging, I suppose.

I blink my eyes open. It's dark outside and Mum's sound asleep. I slide off the settee and go quiet as I can through to the kitchen. I nip out the back door because it doesn't squeak like the front one and slip out into the night.

In the garden it's dark black. The air's soft and the sea's far out; I can tell by the faraway sound it makes. And in the sky there's millions of stars, twinkling away like the shops at Christmas. I stand staring up at them, and see they're moving: little beating hearts of stars. Some of them are tiny, and one is huge and bright, and there are loads and loads of little faint ones flickering away.

Some flying bug brushes past my face and I'm off, pushing through the gate and running down the hillside to Rosa's and the light. Faster and faster I go, down the path, across the road, into the street light, checking for cars as I cross, puffing and panting up to Rosa's door. I hammer with the knocker. Through the letter box I see the inside door open and it's Jim:

"Effie! What're you doing here?"

I follow him through the hall into the back room, blue in the glow from the TV.

Rosa gets up, smoothing down her hair. "Effie! It's late; where's your mum?"

She's cross, I can tell. And I think of what Mum said. Is our welcome all worn out?

Then that crease is back between Rosa's eyes, and she puts her arms round me and she's saying over and over, "What's wrong? What's wrong?"

"Nothing," I tell her, "there's nothing wrong. I just came to see you."

And she's going on about the time again, how late it is, and I'm looking around for Luke and I can't see him.

"Where's Luke?" I ask, when I next get a word in.

"Luke?" she says, as if I'm daft. "In bed, of course." She goes into the kitchen and gets some coats. "Which is where you should be." She puts a coat round my shoulders; it's much too big and it falls off.

"I'll take her back," says Jim.

"I need to go to the toilet first," I say. It's true really.

The toilet's upstairs, and so are the bedrooms. Up I go, straight past the toilet, and quick as anything I open the door to Luke's room and peep inside.

A small computer sits humming away on a tiny desk. The curtains are open, the window is too, just a bit, and the street light shines right in. His bed is flat and empty.

I back out, gently pulling the door shut. Jim and Rosa are downstairs going on and on at each other in loud whispers. Now Bee's starting up from across the hall. I creep back to the bathroom and I'm wondering about Luke and his friends, wondering where he's gone and if Rosa and Jim know. I bet they don't.

There's tapping on the door.

"Hurry up, Effie. It's very late," Rosa whispers from outside.

I finish and pull up my pants. I'll keep Luke's secret. But I'll make him tell me what it is.

I go downstairs and let Jim take me home.

Seven

I wake up to the smell of coffee. I stretch my arms above my head and it hurts. My whole body is sore from digging. I wonder why dogs dig so much – don't they get aches and pains?

I go into Mum's room. She's sitting in bed with her old pink cardigan on, holding a mug in both hands. The sun streams in through the open window, and every time the wind blows the little cobwebby things dance and jump about.

I plonk myself down on the bed next to her.

"Effie!" she grumbles. "Mind my coffee."

I ignore that and snuggle up as close as I can get. "Let's do something. Let's go to the beach.

Show me the places you used to go."

She's staring out at the big blue sky, like she hasn't heard me.

"So, you've met Raine," is all she says.

It's not really a question, but it seems like she wants an answer. I just nod.

"What do you think?" she asks.

"She's like the Ice Queen," I say. "The Ice Queen – or the Witch from Narnia."

Mum snorts, a kind of laugh. "That's why I ran away," she says. "I left home – and Raine won't forgive me." Mum tells me again the story of how, on her sixteenth birthday, she ran away from home, how she got on a boat to the mainland and started a new life. I've heard it loads of times before but this time it's different. Now I've seen Raine and the island Mum left for good – until now.

I get the Narnia book I've had since I was six years old and we look at the black-and-white drawings of the White Witch sitting on her sledge. After a bit Mum says it's made her want to do some sketching, so I fetch her drawing book from her bag on the floor and some of her thick artist's pencils. She gets up, wrapped in her duvet, and sits on the windowsill and soon she's drawing away, with her tongue stuck out one side of her mouth, concentrating.

Mum can concentrate for ages.

I go down to the kitchen and something's wrapping itself round my legs. It's Shadow.

"You'll come and explore with me, won't you, Shadow?"

He just purrs a happy purr.

Mum's mobile's ringing, up in her room, and she starts talking to someone. Then I hear the bathroom taps running.

In a bit, Mum comes into the kitchen. "Better get ready," she says, "it's such a lovely day, we're going for a swim with Rosa and Luke."

"But what about your drawing?"

She doesn't answer me.

That's the thing with my mum; she changes. Half the time she's sad or in a mood or drinking wine. You never know what to expect.

Rosa, Mum, Luke and me go down to the beach near Crow House. Rosa's given us swimsuits and Luke's in his baggy white swim trunks. When he pulls off his tee shirt, there's something round his neck on a piece of leather and I know it's a sea-bead.

The waves roar and crash, galloping up the beach and away again, dragging lumps of seaweed onto the sand.

The sea's angry and loud.

Luke heads straight towards it and plunges in.

There aren't many people on the beach, just two families and an old grandpa paddling about in a rock pool. Most people are in the sea.

"Be careful, the tide's coming in," warns Rosa, shouting above the noise.

"Whee! Let's jump the waves!" Mum grabs my hand and Rosa's hand and pulls us both in.

The cold is shocking. My whole body shudders; I'm shivering and shaking, up to my waist in powerful, cold sea. Bits of black seaweed smack against my legs. I dig my heels into the sand and stones, trying to keep standing. A wave hits my chest. My heart thumps.

Mum drops my hand and dives in. "Mum!" I shout but she's not listening. Sometimes it's like she forgets about me. She swims out, arm over arm, in the swirling blue-green. Rosa laughs and swims away after her.

Mum, Luke and Rosa play around in the water, leaping high then disappearing, their sea-beads banging up and down on their necks.

I stand watching, my feet sinking and shifting deep in the moving sand. There's a cold pain in my head, like when you eat ice cream.

Another big wave comes, I feel myself wobble and I try to shuffle backwards. I want to run, but the sand is dragging me down and the sea is pulling me deeper with giant invisible arms. It's horrible.

"Effie! Come on!" Luke breaks up through the foam right in front of me, his wet hair smooth against his head.

"It's great," I say, pretending to splash about like the others. I'm freezing; my skin's all goose pimples. My teeth are chattering and I can't make them stop. I just want to get away.

A massive wave rolls towards us. I fall. I'm down, fighting, splashing, struggling. My head goes under and I'm gulping salty sea. The wave is pulling me away from the beach. My heart is leaping out of me.

Luke's got my arm. I get on my feet again,

though my legs are like jelly, and we stand together, water swirling round our ankles.

"You can't swim!" he says, like I'm stupid, like it's the worst secret in the world.

I glare at him.

"'Course I can," I lie.

Water's in my ears, it's running down my face. Snot pours down my nose.

I turn and run up the beach to find a towel.

By the time I'm dressed, the weather's changed. The sky's black and heavy now and, just like that, huge drops of rain come pelting down. Everyone on the beach grabs their stuff and makes a run for it.

The waves are rolling about, dark grey with creamy foam, leaping high as a house and smacking – *BOOF* – against the rocks. Mum, Rosa and Luke race up the beach towards me, shouting for clothes and towels.

"Quick!" calls Rosa. "Into the café. Come on." And she's dashing across the little road and I'm running after her.

We squeeze through the café door with loads

of other people, all sheltering from the rain. It's hot in here, there's no room to move. People are trying to towel themselves dry, or climb out of wet clothes, and flicking rain everywhere. I'm squashed against a fat man in a yellow raincoat, and his arm's knocking me in the face. His little round glasses are steamed up and he's wiping them, saying, "Some bloody holiday this is."

We wait ages for somewhere to sit. Mum keeps looking at the red clock on the wall. Suddenly she says she's got to go: "Raine's coming at twelve – I'd better not be late." She gets up, grabs her wet things and heads for the door.

"What about Effie?" Rosa calls.

"Oh, she knows her way by now," says Mum, giving us a little wave, and she's gone.

Sometimes it's like she just doesn't care.

In the end we get the best table, right next to the window, and Rosa gets us some drinks. I've got a hot chocolate in a big yellow mug. The milk's all swirly on top, and I'm sipping it off my spoon, drinking it as slow as I can, making it last.

Luke's next to me. His hair is a black helmet,

wet with rain and sea, with tiny white grains of sand sticking to his cheek. Rosa takes his wet things and puts them over the back of a chair. She smiles across at him and he gives a quick grin back.

For one second, I wish Rosa was my mum. I jab my spoon in the bowl of sugar and twist. I can feel all the tiny grains cracking under the spoon. I twist it round and round, digging a hole, as if I'm digging on the beach. Some of the sugar on top makes brown clumps, where it's wet from my spoon. I push harder until I'm down to the bottom of the bowl. Jab, twist, crunch. Sugar starts spilling out the top and onto the wooden table.

"Effie!" says Rosa. "Don't do that. Please." And she gives me a long old stare like she's looking inside my head.

Rosa turns back to Luke and asks about the fishing boats.

"Was it a good catch today? Are you going down later?" she says to him.

And Luke's telling her, drinking his hot chocolate in quick, greedy gulps.

One happy family. And no room for me.

I say loudly, "Luke wasn't in his bed last night."

Rosa and Luke both look at me.

"What?" says Rosa.

I say it again, a bit quieter this time. I can feel my face going red and hot. Luke dips his head. His face is red too, dark red on his tanned skin.

"What does she mean, Luke?" says Rosa, her voice all pinched up.

He says nothing. My heart is pumping like it's in my head. I wish I could just grab up my words and stuff them back inside.

At last Luke looks up, at Rosa. "I went out for a bit," he tells her.

"What d'you mean? Out – where?" she asks. And she's mad, really mad. Her voice is boiling now, like quiet shouting, and she's glaring across the table at Luke. "What's the matter that you have to sneak out at night without telling me? What's going on?"

"I went down to the quay – with Tom and the others. That's all. Sorry," he mumbles.

"We'll talk about this later. OK?" she tells him.

"OK," he says.

Rosa gets up and pushes past me, going to pay the bill.

"Thanks for nothing," says Luke, standing up, shoving his chair against the table so hard it rocks. He walks away.

I sit at the table and look down at the mess of sugar.

Eight

We don't say much on the way back up the hill. The rain's coming down again, all misty-grey, and we've got our hoods up. Luke goes in front and I walk behind with Rosa. When he reaches his street, Luke goes faster, past the alley, ignoring me, and Rosa carries on after him.

"Bye," she calls.

"Thanks for the hot chocolate!" I shout back, into the rain. No one hears and as I dip into the alley, away from them, I want to say sorry but I don't know how.

Instead I walk up the bank to Crow House, slipping and sliding on the wet grass.

It's the first time it's really rained since we've come here, and now it won't stop. I lift up my face and cold, wet trickles run down inside my fleece. As I get nearer, I can hear voices. I go round the back way and push open the kitchen door. Mum's at the table, and sitting there chatting – in our kitchen – is Raine.

She turns and looks at me. She's got a big dark-green raincoat on, like a farmer. "So, Effie, you've found out that our island isn't always sunny," and she bark-laughs, as if she's made a joke.

I'm standing, dripping, on the doormat.

I go in, pulling off my fleece and kicking off my trainers, making a wet pile by the back door.

"Raine's just been telling me to get a job," says Mum. Her voice is weird – too loud and a bit posh. The voice she uses on the phone.

Raine pushes back her chair. "I was making a *suggestion*. They're looking for help at the craft shop, three days a week."

"A shop assistant," says Mum, ever so quiet.

Raine smiles a slow red smile and taps her nails on the table.

Suddenly I'm shouting: "My mum's an

ARTIST! She's got a job. So don't you come here bossing us about …."

Raine's on her feet, glaring at me; her voice is cold and scary: "I will come here bossing you about, Effie, because this is my house you're living in and my bed you're sleeping in. And your mother should teach you some manners." She looks at Mum: "Think about it, Penny," she says, and she goes out the back door, slamming it hard behind her, letting the rain blow in.

"You've done it now, Effie," Mum tells me. Her hair's all fluffy, like she's just got out of bed, and she's wearing that old pink cardigan over her pyjama bottoms. She pulls it tight round herself and crosses her arms, hugging herself.

I go over and put my arms round her and squeeze as hard as I can. I breathe in her minty smell.

"Better start looking for some work, I suppose," she says, pulling away, "something I want to do."

"What sort of work?"

She thinks for a bit. "Not sure. A hotel, maybe. Reception work. There's bound to be something."

Mum goes upstairs to get changed.

My stomach is growling so I make myself some lunch: sandwiches thick with chocolate spread. I carry the food into the front room and curl up on the sofa with Shadow for company. I feed him pieces of chocolate bread and he chews them up on one side of his mouth. Sometimes they get stuck on his fur and he shakes them off with little nods of his head. I rub him behind his ears and under his chin, over and over, as I'm working out what to do.

Mum calls out: "Bye! Wish me luck!"

I take another bite of sandwich, feeling the chocolate squidge, sweet and heavy, in my mouth. I go over to the big window, striped with rain. Through it I watch Mum pull up her hood and run down the path, the rain coming down on her cats and dogs. And all the time I'm thinking, Don't worry, Mum, don't worry.

I'll get us enough money to live wherever we like.

I search around Crow House for something to dig with. There's no spade anywhere, not even buried under all that junk in the garden and I'm soaking wet again by the time I get back indoors. In the kitchen, I pull open every cupboard, finding all sorts of things: big metal pans, bowls, plates, egg cups and lots of old, empty tins. Useless. A spoon will just have to do. I take the biggest one I can find and shove it in my pocket.

I find some dry clothes and, as soon as the rain stops, I'm out the door, snaking through the wet grass towards Crow Head. The path is skiddy-wet under my feet; I nearly fall flat on my face. Everything out here smells sweet and new and full of the countryside, just like on the shampoo adverts.

It's a lot easier this time to find the digging place. I zoom straight to it and sink to my knees. The ground's cold, oozy with mud; there's dark patches of wet on the knees of my jeans. I can work faster with the spoon, and soon I'm down to where I was last time, scuffing up roots and stones and two black, shiny beetles. But it's still no good; the massive rock won't budge more than a cat's whisker of a millimetre.

A wind starts up; I pull my fleece tight round me and zipper it together. The sky's dark again – more rain coming, I suppose. I begin to scoop the earth back into the hole, covering it up, pressing the soft soil down. As the first raindrops hit the back of my neck, I think I see something shining: just a glint. I get down on my knees and wriggle my hands into the earth, searching with the tips of my fingers.

Got it: it's cold, made of metal. I close my fingers around it and pull. Whatever the thing is, it's stuck fast. I keep good hold of it and wriggle it about. My stomach's doing butterflies.

Suddenly out it comes, a great ball of twisty metal and soil. It springs into shape in my hands, showering soil: a heavy bracelet, made of lots of golden strings all twisted together, like rope. Amazing! At each end is a fierce bird's head, with red jewel eyes, the same as on my brooch. I slip my arm inside it – up to my shoulder. It's giant size and it weighs a ton. My heart is banging and jumping about, I'm so excited. This is better than anything I've seen on telly, like the Crown Jewels or something. Better even – 'cos I found it.

And how much more of this stuff is down there?

I twist the bracelet round and round on my

arm, then take it in my hands again to knock off the dirt, rubbing it, cleaning it up. It's definitely gold.

More rain falls: hard, heavy drops, faster and faster. I shove the bracelet up inside my top and stamp down the earth.

Digging's over, for today, but I'm more sure than ever there's a whole load of treasure just waiting for me to find.

I race home, the rain pouring buckets on my head and the bracelet joggling up and down inside my tee shirt. I hold my arms flat against my sides to keep it safe. I bet Luke would like to see this.

Back at Crow House I go straight to the bathroom and take out the bracelet. Little bits of earth drop off all over the floor. I run some water in the bath and carefully put the bracelet in, watching it sink to the very bottom. Kneeling down to reach, I wipe it with my flannel to get off all the mud, just like I did with the brooch. Now I can see it properly, I'm even more certain it's gold, but it's much too big to go round someone's arm. When all the muck is off, I pull out the bath plug and lift the bracelet out, careful not to drop it. I put a towel round it and carry it into my room.

It's really early when I go to bed. I lie awake for ages listening to the TV from downstairs: a muddle of voices, crazy laughter, cheers and claps. Mum's watching her favourite show. Through my window, the sky is dark purple-grey. I wonder what Luke's doing? What if I've got him grounded? Will he ever speak to me again?

The bracelet is underneath my pillow with the brooch. I reach my hand under and touch them again with my fingertips, wondering who hid them up at Gull Head.

I think about treasure – heaps of it, my pockets full to bursting with shiny golden coins. I just know it's there. The problem is, how do I get it out?

When I close my eyes, all I can see is flat, black rock and dark, dark earth. And Luke's face, with a sharp eagle eye, glaring at me.

Nine

All night I'm tossing and turning. I keep waking up to check the bracelet and brooch. In my dreams I see Luke's face, cross and scowly, looking daggers at me.

Next morning my head aches. I pull out the bracelet and examine it, feeling it heavy in my lap. With my dirty tee shirt I rub off some of the bits of soil still caught around the birds' heads. I try it again on my arm, even though you could get about three people's arms inside. All the time I'm thinking of Luke and Rosa. Are they still angry with me?

I put the bracelet back inside my pillowcase

and throw the tee shirt on the wash pile in the corner. Then I pull on my clothes and run downstairs. There's one slice of bread left so I grab that and hurry into the garden. Shadow will have to wait for breakfast; I'm off to Rosa's.

From up here on the hill, I can see all the way down to the harbour; the sunshine twinkling on the boats as they chug out to sea. As I run, I make bets with myself: If I can make it to the next bush before that boat goes round the headland, everything will be all right.

Jim opens the door. He's wearing his dark blue fisherman's jersey with the sleeves rolled up. Behind him, in the kitchen, Luke's sitting at the table but he doesn't come out to say hello.

"Rosa's down at the shop this morning," Jim says.

I bite my lip, hoping he won't shut the door on me.

"Go along and see her, if you like. Maybe you can help to look after Bee?" Jim gives me a wink.

I've never been to Rosa's shop before, so Jim comes with me. It isn't far; past the wiggly railings, down the little road with the garage on the corner. The shop is tiny, wedged in between a house and a locked-up shed, with bright blue windowsills and red flowers in pots outside.

Ask for the Moon

it says in big blue letters right across the doorway, and underneath:

Everything you need for your Island Holiday
Open

"I'll leave you to it," says Jim.

I push open the door and a bell pings. I can hear Bee going *dah-dah-dah* and Rosa's head bobs up from behind the counter.

"Effie! How are you this morning?" She's smiling and I smile back. Phew.

"Ping!" goes the bell again. It's customers – a little kid and his mum – so Rosa starts talking to them.

I look around. The shop is stuffed full of all kinds of things. There's rails with clothes on, starting from tiny children's coats, getting bigger and longer 'til they're adults' clothes; dresses, jeans, all sorts. Hanging from the ceiling is a massive fisherman's net and dangling down from it are kites, fishing rods and rubbery diving suits. On the floor, there's lots of wooden boxes, like the ones down at the harbour, with piles of things inside: two are full of wellies, another is a jumble of buckets and spades, and one box has just got umbrellas sticking out – red, black, blue and spotty, some long ones with points on and other smaller ones, the fold-up kind. I'm keeping an eye out for something to dig with but all the spades are rubbishy plastic.

The little boy is at the bucket-and-spade box, pulling them all out over the wooden floor.

"Hurry up, Ben," says the woman. "Just choose one."

He waddles over to the counter with a red bucket, shaped like a castle, and his mum gives Rosa the money. She buys two books for herself at the same time.

"What a wonderful shop," she tells Rosa. "You sell everything!"

"Everything you need for a holiday – whatever the weather," says Rosa. "You can buy your tickets here too – boat trips, fishing trips, trips to Seal Island." She points to a board behind the counter with pictures of them all.

"We'll definitely be back," the woman says.

Rosa comes out from behind the counter and starts to tidy up the buckets and spades. Bee crawls out after her. She sees me and grabs my leg.

"What do you think of our shop?" Rosa's finished tidying and she's looking at me. "It's our first season."

"It's AMAZING," I say, tickling Bee's tummy.

"It is, isn't it?" She gives me a massive smile. "Most people come on holiday without something. They can pick it up here for next to nothing; it's all second-hand stuff."

"Where does it come from?"

"Lots of it gets left behind – in B&Bs, cafés, down on the beach. We keep it for a few months and if no one claims it, we sell it. Some things have been given to me by neighbours. All good as new."

Rosa looks round, like she's queen of it all.

"We open three mornings a week. It makes a bit of extra money."

I help Rosa the whole morning. At lunchtime,

we clear the counter and pack away; Rosa puts
Bee in the buggy then turns the sign on the
door to

Closed

"Let's go and get some lunch!" she says. "I've got
some garlic bread at home."

Bliss.

In the afternoon, I'm sitting at Rosa's kitchen
table writing out price tickets. I do a ticket for
every single amount I can think of up to fifty
pounds. Rosa says she never gets anything worth
more than that.

"It's not a posh shop, just a shop for ordinary
people on holiday," she tells me.

"Why is it called Ask for the Moon?"

"Well, it's a joke, because of my name … Rosa
Moon."

Duh. I know that.

"It's an old saying," Rosa goes on. "It means to
ask for something which you're not likely to get."

"But you CAN get it – your shop sells nearly
everything!"

"Exactly," she says. "That's the joke."

"I'd call my shop Effie's Emporium," I tell her, pushing the lid back on my felt-tip. "A shop full of mystery and excitement."

The front door swings open and Luke comes in. I feel myself go red and I don't really know what to say.

"Hello," I manage.

Is he still angry with me?

Luke just nods and slips into his chair on the other side of the table. He's been down the harbour; his jumper's all damp and smelly.

"What're you doing?" he asks.

I show him the price tickets.

"If you had a shop, what would you call it?" Rosa asks him.

"Depends on what I was selling," he says.

"Fish," I say.

"The Fish Shop," says Luke. "Then everyone knows where they are."

"They could probably tell anyway," says Rosa. "One whiff of you and –"

"OK, OK, I'll go and get a shower!" Luke gets up, pulls the smelly blue jumper over his head and makes for the stairs. "See you, Effie."

"See you."

Inside I'm smiling.

Then I stand up and give Rosa a hug, just because I can.

"I thought Luke wouldn't speak to me again," I whisper into her dress.

"He's giving you a second chance. Everyone deserves that." Rosa looks down at me. "Even Raine, don't you think?"

"What?" I'm amazed. "But she's horrible – don't you know why Mum ran away? Raine was a mean mother. All the rules and punishments, Mum couldn't stand it. I'm on Mum's side."

Rosa nods her head. "Yes, I know, Effie, but that was a long time ago – and everyone makes mistakes, don't they? Can't you try to get to know Raine a little bit? You might even get to like her."

Ten

So Rosa fixes it up and we get invited to tea at Raine's house.

We trail along a dusty road, Rosa in front and me dragging behind. The sun's beating down on my head and my hair's prickly with it. I've got a stone in my trainer and it's digging hard on the bone of my heel.

"Come on, Effie. Not long now," Rosa calls, pushing the buggy with Bee fast asleep.

I go even slower, poking at my heel with my finger. It's no good. I sit down, right in the middle of the road, and kick off my shoe. There's no cars anyway. And no real, big noise except the great roaring, rushing sound of the sea.

Rosa's stopped and I know she's watching me.

"Hurry up now, Effie, you agreed to come. We're late enough already."

I look up at her tired face and feel bad because she's right. But I wish I was on a windy cliff-top, digging for gold, not walking for ages down this hot old road in the blazing sunshine.

Rosa turns and carries on again without me, so I hurry to catch her up.

We turn a corner and she points.

"There's Raine's house, in the trees."

I see it, a big stone house like Crow House but without the sun. The trees hang round it like curtains on the stage. It's shady and dark and a bit creepy too. We get to the front of the house, to a massive iron gate with a stone post each side.

There's a green, whispery silence.

I want to run, but Rosa is talking at me.

"It's called Eel Cottage, though it's a house really. Ages ago, it belonged to the gamekeeper who looked after the big manor – that's empty now and all locked up. Raine's here all alone."

Then everything's happening too fast. Rosa's leaning forwards over the buggy, she's pushing open the black gate and Bee's awake, making a fuss. Rosa goes up to the door and presses on the bell.

I stand just behind them, listening to Raine's footsteps stomping inside the house.

And there she is, scowling like some cross teacher. "Come in," she says. Her ice-eyes glitter.

"Go on," Rosa tells me.

I go over the doorstep and my mouth's as dry as toast. I'm blinking because it's dark in here, dark and cold. When I can see properly again, I'm in a square hallway. The walls are covered with stuff: old paintings of people in hats stare down at me, next to wooden masks with grinning mouths. There's horns from a dead animal stuck over the doorway in front of me and, in the fireplace, where the fire should be, there's a vase of dried-up flowers. I can smell dust and deadness everywhere. There's no sound except the slow *tock, tock* of the thin black clock on the mantelpiece.

I want to run back outside to the sunshine but I know she's watching me, waiting.

My hair's slipped out its elastic bands and keeps flopping in my eyes. I push it away and stare right into her face.

"Sorry if I was rude to you," I say in my most

un-sorry voice.

Raine gives a sharp laugh, like a cough, and goes through the doorway with the horns. I go after her.

In the next room, it's light again. There's a long, shiny table covered with old-fashioned tea things, like in a posh doll's house, only real size. There's plates full of cakes and sandwiches and, right in the middle, a huge, brown teapot. Raine lifts the pot with one hand and holds it over a cup.

"Do you drink tea?" she asks.

I nod, though I don't really. She pushes the cup in its saucer across the shiny table towards me and I sit down in one of the old wooden chairs. I'm as far away from her as I can get. My heart's slowed down a bit now, though I sit crooked in the chair keeping one foot on the floor, ready to run. Where's Rosa?

I stare hard at Raine. My mother's mother. I try to see some part of Mum's face in hers but I can't.

Rosa and Bee come in and the room turns noisy and normal. Bee sits on Rosa's lap and reaches out for the food. She grabs a cake and squeezes it hard in her fist until it's a jammy, sticky mess.

Those long cakes with the chocolate are lovely but I won't eat a thing. I'm still on Mum's side.

All through the tea, Rosa keeps on at me: "Why don't you eat something, Effie? Look, éclairs!" And she shoves the plate of cakes at me.

I don't give in. Raine gives me a witchy stare; her eyes are sharp as knives.

"Don't force her, Rosa," Raine says, "she isn't used to me yet." She gives that little cough-laugh again. Then, wicked as you like, she goes: "Effie, help me clear the plates away, please."

She wants to get me on my own.

I sit still, like a statue.

Rosa's staring at me now, so I push back my chair. With a pile of sticky plates and two teacups balanced on top, I follow Raine down a little passage into the kitchen.

It isn't old-fashioned in here, not like the other rooms. There's a fridge, a round table and a shiny silver sink. Raine's smiling at me.

I'm standing in the middle of the kitchen, arms full of plates, when I see them.

On the draining board there are bones – long, thin, white ones – and the skeleton of a tiny *hand*.

My heart starts up a fast pitter-pat. Behind the sink, on the windowsill, sits a grinning skull – with teeth.

"What are all these? Why are they here?" I ask. I dump the plates on the table and get up close to the sink for a better look.

"Didn't your mother tell you? I'm an archaeologist." Raine stands next to me. "Bones are all part of the job."

"Not in a kitchen," I say.

And Raine laughs again, a proper one this time, with her head thrown back. "Perhaps not." Then she gets all serious again. "These are all waiting for another archaeologist to examine: a bone expert. I'm more interested in the objects people left behind."

"What sort of objects?" I want to know. I'm thinking about brooches and bracelets and buried treasure. I bet she'd be interested in those!

Raine's eyes are shining. "Pottery, coins, pieces of glass; all the things that give us clues about how people lived long ago. Shall I tell you a secret? I think I've found something really exciting: a Roman villa. We've just begun the dig."

"A real dig, like on the telly?"

Raine nods.

Brilliant. A dig means tools – like spades and stuff; things I can take up to Gull Head. "Can I come?" I ask.

"I don't see why not," Raine says. "You can come along on Friday."

And later, when we're all sitting round Rosa's table, pushing hot, red tomatoey spaghetti into our mouths, I tell everyone about the dig. "Have you been on a proper dig with Raine?" I ask Luke, twirling up a massive, juicy forkful. "Has my mum? Why didn't she tell me that's what Raine does?"

"We didn't know you'd be so keen," says Rosa.

"It's about time someone showed you the Bone Cave, I think," says Jim. "Maybe Luke will bring you down?"

I have so many questions; they're fighting to get out past the spaghetti. All I manage is, "Let's go!"

Luke gives me his crooked grin. "It's shut now, Donkey. We'll go tomorrow."

Donkey! Just for that, I grab the last piece of garlic bread.

Eleven

I don't get a wink of sleep. In the morning at Gull Head, the sun is just coming up from the sea. The whole sky is orangey-yellow. I reckon it's really early but I'm too excited to stay in bed. The gold. A Bone Cave. And a dig. This island just gets better.

My trainers leave a maze of misty footprints across the wet, springy grass. The fat old gulls are sitting on their nests yelling at me but they don't really mind me now – and I don't mind them. I've got the spoon in my pocket, ready for a dig of my own.

As soon as I get to the place I know someone's been here. The grass and heather's all torn up and scraggy-looking; I'd never leave it like this in a million years. I fall onto my knees and scoop away the soil. Stones and earth come up quick and easy; everything feels a bit different.

"Effie! Effie! I know you're here." It's Luke, running along the cliff path.

I fall flat on my face in the grass, hoping he won't see me. My heart is beating like crazy.

"EFFIE, IF YOU WANT TO SEE THE BONE CAVE COME ON!"

Luke's yelling now and the gulls are screeching too. Maybe it's Luke who's been here? Maybe he knows about the gold anyway? I keep my head down. I want to get this treasure on my own.

The gulls are screaming and whirling about all over the place, getting frantic. I make myself as flat as I can, pressing my face into the scratchy heather as I wait for Luke to run up to me. Any minute he'll find me. But he doesn't come. At last I lift my head and risk a look: he's gone.

I'll have to cover up the hole and come back later, after I've been to the cave.

I tear at tufts of heather and grass and stuff them down into the hole. I wobble the rock again, just to test it. And the rock comes loose. I stretch out and hug it with both arms. I push it and pull it and it shifts, backwards and forwards, side to side. Suddenly the rock lurches and there's a gap big enough for me to put one arm in.

I push my arm down and feel around in the cold soil. There's a kind of underground wall made of flat stones. It feels like a tunnel – a proper tunnel someone's made, going down behind the rock. I think about all the people I've ever seen trapped in tunnels on the News. People it takes days to rescue – and some who never get rescued at all. I know I shouldn't go in there.

But of course I know I will.

Luke opens the door on the first ring, still cool and salty from the outside air.

"Where've you been?" he says, screwing up his eyes in the sunlight. "Didn't you hear me calling? Are you up to something?"

"Are *you*?" I ask him. I push my hair out of my face and bits of heather and earth drop down the front of my tee shirt.

He just looks at me. I wonder what he's thinking.

"Are we going to the Bone Cave, then?" I say.

Luke pulls the front door closed behind him and off we go, across the road and through the alley.

"Bet you've not seen a cave this good before. They don't have caves in the city."

"'Course they do, massive ones," I say, lying through my teeth. "They run right under the streets, next to the sewers."

We go up the hill, past Crow House, and Luke heads off along the same cliff path again. Far below us the white, foamy waves crash against the rocks, making a lion's roar of noise.

The grass under our feet changes to that short, springy stuff; this is the way to my digging place. I slow down a little bit. Does Luke know about the gold, somehow? Is he teasing me?

Just when I'm sure of it, he dodges off the path, into the bushes. There's stone steps made in the rock and he's scuffling down them. He's fast. I scramble down too, sending loose stones bouncing into the trees.

"Watch it! It's dangerous!" he shouts, turning

round. "Hold the handrail."

And I see a wooden railing running down along the steps so I grab it with one hand, just to shut him up. We're away from the sea and the wind now; it's green and silent in here with the sun shining in through the trees, making patterns. It's warm, too warm. I open my fleece but there's no time to pull it off, we're running, slipping, sliding, and I'm hanging on the rail with both hands. Tiny black flies buzz round my head. It's hard to breathe.

Luke skids to a stop.

The steps have disappeared; there's a smooth path, and a sign on a tree with a painted arrow.

It says:

BONE CAVE THIS WAY

Luke twists through a little wooden gate. I'm right next to him. And here it is: a proper arched cave in the hillside. At the entrance is a kind of shop counter and a till, and sitting behind them is Jim. Bee's here too, standing up on his knee, holding out her arms to Luke.

Luke goes up to her and gives her a tickle

on her fat little belly, and she squeals, happy as anything to see him.

"There you are!" says Jim. "I thought you'd forgotten." He stands up and throws Bee onto his shoulder. He's holding out some keys.

"Before you go, Effie wants to see inside," Luke tells him.

"Sure. Don't be long, though – and helmets, remember." Jim points to the wall where rows of red and yellow safety helmets are hanging on hooks.

Luke hands me a red one and I cram it on my head, ready to go.

I walk close to Luke into the massive stone O of the cave. Down we go along a wide sloping path, and all the time it's getting a bit darker. Then there's a click; some little lights flicker on the walls and send out a yellow glow. The floor's all smooth earth, and it's really cold now. I can feel the goose pimples all the way up my arms under my fleece.

Luke stops, dead still. There's more lights here. We're in a kind of round room, with curved, rocky walls. And stacked up all around the walls are layers and layers of bones. Piles of them, one on top of the other, neat as anything. There must be hundreds, floor to ceiling. I turn round and around, and everywhere it's the same neat stacks. I go over and put out my hand to feel –

"Don't touch! The whole lot'll come down," Luke says, sounding weird and echoey.

"Are they people's? People's bones?" I'm thinking of the skeleton hand on Raine's drainer.

"Animals," says Luke. "But really, really old ones – reindeer, bison, cave bear – things that haven't been around since the Ice Age." He spins round in the middle of the cave.

"But how did they get here?"

"No one knows. They might have fallen down tunnels or maybe got washed in from other places. These cliffs are full of tunnels, y'know, and sea caves cut out by the waves."

Tunnels. He's having a laugh – he must be.

"Hey!" It's Jim calling us.

"He wants to take Bee home for her nap," says Luke, turning back the way we came. "I look after the place when he's away."

"Does he work here?" I ask.

Luke laughs his cat-laugh. "'Course. He

works for Raine. She owns it and people pay to come here and have a look round. There's a group booked for one o'clock; he wants to get back for that."

Jim and Bee go – and me and Luke are left in charge.

"You'd better see the museum part, and then I've shown you everything," Luke says. "You won't need your helmet in there." He leads the way through another short passageway and we're in a different cave room. This time, there's lots of glass cabinets, like in an ordinary museum. We walk round, peering at the objects. There's some ancient ship's cannon balls and a giant anchor. One cabinet has a load of broken pottery inside with a massive photograph as the background.

"Recognise Raine?" Luke points to a woman in shorts and tough boots, holding up a huge pot and grinning.

I stare hard at her face; she's a lot younger in the photograph and her hair is as red as mine, but you can still see it's her.

"That discovery made her famous," Luke says.

"Famous?"

"Well, famous enough to start up this

museum – and have people visit it from all round the world," he says. "Museum people. Archaeologists, people like that." He moves away to look at a painting of a ship with sails.

Then I see it. In a glass case in the middle of the room is a treasure chest, just like in the movies. Its lid is shut but real gold coins are scattered all around it.

I peer in through the glass. My stomach does a flip of excitement. "Luke, where did they get this? Did they dig it up – here – on the island?"

Luke comes over. "It's a fake – look what it says on the label."

I press my nose against the glass, trying to make out the tiny spidery writing:

Trading ships such as the Royale Merchant, wrecked in the 1600s, carried silver and gold coins and precious stones.
Are chests full of treasure still to be washed up on our shores?

Twelve

There's footsteps. Luke goes back outside and he's talking to someone. I'm staring at all the stuff in the treasure case when Raine comes in.

"Hello, Effie. So you've seen our little museum?" She stands looking at me. "Would you like to have a look at my latest finds? It's too early to put them on display; we need to do a lot more digging and excavating before the general public sees them." Raine goes over to a cupboard at the back of the room and unlocks a drawer.

I'm holding my breath: I'm sure she's going to bring out a pot full of gold.

"Well, come and see, then." She signals me over.

Raine's pulled out a drawer covered with a white cloth. Ever so slowly she folds open the cloth – there's some little plastic bags inside with numbers on. She opens the bags and carefully shakes out two tiny bits of broken pottery, some old green glass and three silver coins with a man's head on. "Now these have come from what I think – I hope – is the Roman villa." She's smiling all over her face.

Not even a speck of gold or jewels; nothing wonderful that I can see. I don't know what to say, but Raine doesn't seem to mind.

"Exciting, isn't it?" she goes on. "It could really put us on the map. There aren't many Roman villas around here, I can tell you." She's all lit up. "But we must wait; wait to see what else comes up when we excavate."

Like some greedy miser, she wraps all her treasures up again and puts them away.

"Can I still come to the dig like you promised?" I ask her.

"Of course. It's quite a way from Crow House but Jim will bring you in the truck. Luke can come along too, if he'd like; he enjoyed himself last time."

It's weird, standing here talking to Raine, after all the bad things Mum's told me about her. I look past her, to the cabinet with the big photograph of her all those years ago, smiling, with long, red hair.

Just then Jim comes back and it's time to go.

"I haven't seen Bee today; I'll go along and pop my head in," Raine says to him.

Luke runs on and me and Raine climb back up the path and through the bushes to the cliff-top, past the front of Crow House then down the grassy hill to the town. I wonder what Mum is doing? Will she mind me talking to Raine? The wind is blowing hard now, battering my head and fighting with Raine's hair, pulling it out of its clips.

"What sort of spades do you use – you know, when you're digging up stuff?" I have to shout so Raine can hear me over the wind.

"We have trowels and lots of other tools too. I'll show you before you start," Raine tells me. "I'm very glad you're interested."

We reach the bottom of the hill and the wind

dies down. It's easier to talk now.

"When I'm teaching people about archaeology, I start by holding up two objects," she says. "A safety helmet and a toothbrush."

I give Raine a look: a *toothbrush*?

"The helmet means 'Keep safe' and the toothbrush means 'Be careful'. Things from the past are very, very precious. We use soft brushes – even tiny toothbrushes – to gently clear the earth from an object so that we don't damage it."

She sounds a bit like a teacher but I don't mind.

"Honestly, Effie, it's a wonderful feeling to dig up an object that belonged to someone thousands of years ago – to think that the last person who touched it may have been a Celt or a Roman. I do hope you have that experience one day."

"What about pirate treasure?" I ask, but Raine's already ringing on Rosa's door and she's not really listening.

If she just knew what I've got in my bedroom. I bet she'd listen then.

Thirteen

It's evening. I'm on my bed looking at my brooch and the bracelet, wondering for the millionth time who they belonged to. Mum's door bangs shut and she creaks along the landing to my room. I slide the things under my pillow.

"Guess what, I've got a job!" She stands in the doorway in a new white top and her best dangly earrings. Her bag is hanging off one shoulder and her hair's all shiny clean. She looks lovely.

"What job?" I ask. "The one at the gift shop?"

"No. As if...!" She laughs so much, the earrings dance about. "I've found my own job, thank you. At the pub, the Rose and Anchor – only three nights a week and half-day on Saturdays. I start tonight." Mum checks her watch. "At seven, so I'd better get a move on."

I look at her. "I'll go back to Rosa's then."

Mum sits on my bed. "Best not, Fee," she says, "you've been there all day." She feels around in her bag for her purse. "Tell you what, here's a bit of money for chips. Run down to the shop and get yourself a nice big bag. See if you can find something good on telly."

With a little wave, she gets up and slips out the door.

I sit and listen to her hurrying down the stairs. The back door closes and I'm alone. I don't really mind being on my own at night; it happened millions of times at our old place. But there was always someone about: kids on the stairs, Mrs Vashi next door cooking curries and shouting at her mother down the phone. Here there's just the wind.

I go to the window and look out. Maybe Shadow will come for a visit? Crow House creaks and sighs and the trees outside shuffle their branches. I wonder if this place really is haunted. A cold little shiver runs up the back of my neck. I wish Luke hadn't said anything about all that. Stupid boys.

I go back to bed and snuggle under the duvet, cuddling down. I think I'll just go to sleep — then it will be morning and Mum will be home.

When I wake up it's dark and I'm starving hungry. I feel for the lamp and switch it on. The clock says it's nearly half past ten. I scramble out of bed, pull on my hoodie and pick up the coins Mum left. If I hurry, I'll catch the chippie before it shuts.

In the kitchen, I put on my trainers and go out the back way, carefully turning the key in the lock and stuffing it deep in my pocket. I keep a lookout for Shadow as I run down the garden and along the path to the town.

I can smell the chip shop from the corner of the street. There's no one else inside, so I don't have to wait long. The chip man has a round, spotty face and he's sweaty from cooking. He gives me a massive helping and lets me put the vinegar on myself, 'til the plastic box is wet at the bottom.

"You must be Jim's niece?" he says, as he wraps up my chips. "Raine's granddaughter, eh? You have a look of her about you."

"I'm Penny's daughter," I say, handing over the money. When I get outside, I glare at him through the steamed-up glass.

The chips are warm in my hands and I hurry off down to the harbour. I find a wooden seat and sit swinging my legs, cramming the squelchy chips into my mouth, looking out to sea. There's a round, white moon hanging in the sky. The wind's gone now and the sea's quiet tonight, quiet and still. The lights from all the houses higher up the bay shine on the dark water. The bobbing fishing boats send out silvery snail-trails of light.

I eat the very last chip, fold up the wrapper and put it in the bin. I suck my fingers clean and think about what to do. I could go and meet Mum from her job. I know where the Rose and Anchor is – it's that big pub down on the front, next to the tea room. I'm not sure that's a good idea though; I'm well underage. But maybe it's different if your mum works there.

I run along the seafront to the pub. There's no

one much about; all the little shops and cafés are dark and closed for the night.

The Rose and Anchor's got tables outside where families have their pub lunches in the daytime. A few people are sitting out now, drinking and chatting, and I go past them up to the open door. It's noisy and crowded inside. There's loads of men standing in the doorway, drinking pints of beer and laughing. One of them turns round and some of his beer drips onto my jeans.

"Sorry, darling," he says. He gives a massive burp.

I take a step backwards. Mum might be busy, anyway. Maybe I can see her through a window? I go down past the tables again and cut round the back to the little yard with the big rubbish bins. It's dark here and a huge fan is whirring, blowing out hot garlic air. There's no window so I can't see in.

I go back to the street, dodging past some teenagers having a snog. This is the modern part of town, I remember Jim telling us as he drove us through. It's nothing like a big city but the road's been paved over for people to walk on, there's a kids' play park and a concrete hump for skateboarding. Behind is a line of streetlights, and a high, curved wall with the beach on the other side. The play park is empty and full of shadows, only lit by one street lamp and the glow of the moon. I sit on a swing and drag my feet backwards and forwards.

Just then, from out of the shadows jump some dark figures. I stop swinging and sit like a statue, watching. More and more of them come towards me; I count eleven bodies, twisting and turning in fast flips and somersaults, silent as cats. They're boys, boys about Luke's age, doing a weird kind of dance across the concrete. They don't see me. They flip and bound, rolling and curling themselves like they're in a gym. Up the wall they go, flinging their bodies over the top, onto the beach. One boy crouches on top of the wall for a moment, straightens up and throws himself forwards. I see his long straight hair and skinny body outlined against the sky. Luke. This is his secret.

Straightaway I follow them. The wall's too high for me so I have to snake round it, almost back to the pub. I stay in the shadow of the wall and creep over the sand towards the boys. What are they doing? They've spread out now across the beach, rolling and twisting and bending in the light of the moon, moving further away from the town and the park. They're going towards the darkness at the top end of the beach, towards the boulders and rocks, with the high cliffs behind.

They're like animals; they leap like tigers and run like the fastest cheetahs. It's hard to keep up. I cling to the shelter of the wall, stumbling and tripping, keeping my eyes fixed on them, trying to stay invisible. They've reached the rocks now and they fan out, springing upwards, crouching, balancing, gliding like birds. The only sound is the sigh of the sea.

Amazing. It's a stunt show circus – and I'm the secret audience.

As if there's been a signal, one by one the boys change direction away from the rocks, flipping their bodies up to the long wall. They're heading back towards me, running along the top of the wall with their arms outstretched for balance. Quick, I should run now before they get too close – but I can't seem to move or look away. Instead, I crouch back further into the shadows.

Nearly all at the same time, they leap off and somersault onto the sand. Luke walks forwards until he's almost in front of me. I can see his eyes glittering in the street light and his tee shirt moving up and down as he breathes. He looks strong and brave. The other boys move to stand behind him. I can't tell if they've seen me or not. I hold my breath and keep very, very still.

There's a burst of laughter from the street.

"Let's have a late-night dip!" someone shouts and there's people running onto the sand, big men acting daft.

The boys scatter, like deer in a nature programme on telly.

I'm left watching the big, drunk men scuffling in the sand, tripping each other up, chasing each other down to the sea.

When I get back up to the street, the Rose and Anchor has closed and people are walking away down along the seafront. I hang around outside but it's ages before I hear Mum's voice.

"Night! See you Saturday," she calls out to someone still inside the pub. At last she comes out, pulling on her denim jacket.

I'm a bit cold too.

She sees me straightaway. "Effie. What are you doing here?"

"I've come to meet you," I say, putting my arm through hers and snuggling up.

I want to tell her about Luke, about the amazing climbing stuff, but I don't. It's his secret – and mine now too.

Mum's in a great mood. She tells me all about the other people who work at the Rose and Anchor. And she tells me about the people who drink there, the *reglars* she calls them, and puts on funny voices, making them real.

We hang on each other's arms all the way home.

"I'm shattered," she says as soon as we get in. "Make sure you don't wake me up in the morning, Effie." And she creaks her way upstairs to bed.

I lie in my bed for hours, full of chips and questions about Luke and his mates. I watch the moon shining in through my window, like a huge flat face.

Fourteen

I'm awake very, very early, before the sun is even in the sky. I can see it, though, just coming up from the sea, making the whole sky pink. The moon is still hanging there, like it wants to stay longer: strange and ghosty-white. I sit up in bed and take my treasures onto my lap. Tiny specks of dry soil sprinkle the duvet like pepper. Blurry with sleep, I rub the giant bracelet gently on the front of my pyjamas, making it shine. Today I will go to the dig and get a trowel, and then go back to Gull Head. My heart is pounding. I'll find a way to get the rest of that treasure.

I will never give up.

The sun's up, shining in through my window when I leap out of bed and pull on shorts and a tee shirt.

"Effie!" It's Luke's voice, loud, coming from down in the kitchen. "Are you ready?"

I scrabble under my bed for my rucksack, swing it onto my shoulder and run downstairs.

Mum's here; she's got the back door wide open and she's standing on the doormat staring at all the green outside. Her nightie flutters against her legs in the breeze.

"Do you want to come with us?" Luke asks her. "Jim said to tell you he's got the truck."

She doesn't say anything. She just keeps staring outside.

"Come on. Come with us," I say.

Mum shakes her head. A little trickle of fear shivers through me. I hope Mum's OK. I hope she isn't getting ill again. Slowly I follow Luke through the back door.

"What's up with your mum?" he asks as we go round the side of the house.

"She gets like that sometimes. Sad and ..." I stop. I don't want to think about Mum's moods today.

"Race you!" I shout, heading off across the grass, and we speed down the hill, side by side.

I can see Jim's blue truck waiting at the bottom.

Luke overtakes me easily, skidding off down the slope, and stands waiting for me near the truck.

We both squeeze in the front with Jim – me in the middle and Luke next to the window. I look at him, wondering if he saw me on the beach spying on him and his monkey friends. It's really hot so we have both windows right down and Jim drives with one brown arm hanging over the side. Every time we bump round a corner, he shouts out, "Still there, everyone?"

We jiggle about like crazy, me and Luke bashing into each other as we swing round the bends. The wind blows my hair all over my face. Trees and hedges smash past us, and bits of leaves and twigs get ripped off and fly into the truck.

At the top of a hill, Jim points to a big field. "We'll park in there," he says. "I can't take us all the way; the road doesn't go that far, so we'll have to walk the last bit. There's a short cut across the next field."

He slows down and pulls on the brake. Luke jumps out and opens a metal gate so we can drive across the grass. Jim parks the truck in the corner under some trees. "Put the window up, Effie," he says, "or the truck will be full of flies on the way home."

Luke catches us up and we all set off across the field and over another gate at the top. The ground near the gate is oozy and soft; it sucks at my feet, squelching and pulling. Soon my trainers are covered in it and there's flicks of brown up my legs.

"You kids should have worn wellies," says Jim.

We race through the next field, me and Luke splashing through the soggy bits. The sun's out hard now, shining on my face, so I have to screw up my eyes to see properly. I can feel the mud drying on my legs, making them itch. Past the next gate, there's a plain brown field of earth with a few people moving about. It's the dig. Jim undoes the metal gate catch and we squeeze through.

"Raine and the others started digging the trench yesterday," he tells us.

As we get nearer, I can see how the earth has been carved up into a massive square hole. Some people are digging at the sides and others are standing down inside. We get right up close before I see one of them is Raine, on her knees in the mud. She looks at us, squinching up her eyes into the sun.

"Hello, Jim," she says, climbing out, "have you brought me some helpers?"

She looks really different from last time. She's got brown shorts on and big lace-up boots like mountain climbers wear, and she's covered in mud. There's even mud on her face. Her voice is still the same, though – hard and posh.

"Are you sure you want to join us, Effie?" She's staring down at me. "You're not afraid of dirty work, are you?"

I shake my head. My heart starts to thump – she's going to send me away before I've had a chance to find out anything useful.

I stand ramming my heels into the mud, staring back. There's no way I'm going home.

Raine makes up her mind. "Let's see what you're made of, then."

And I jump down into the trench.

She shows me all the tools they use. She lifts up a thing with a long wooden handle and sharp metal points at one end. "It's a pickaxe. We use it for digging into hard ground," she tells me.

I grab hold of it – it's heavy – and I swing it down as hard as I can, slicing into the earth.

"Watch out!" Raine shouts. "You can't use that unless you're wearing boots." She pulls the pick away from me and gives me a different kind of tool: a trowel. It's small and light and fits into my hand. Its blade is a metal triangle with a very pointy tip. Perfect.

"You have to be very patient and careful to be a good archaeologist," Raine says. "Everything you find in the trench is precious – a piece in the jigsaw."

We work together for a bit, both scraping away at the earth with our trowels. The sun shines down on us. Raine's face is soon covered with tiny flecks of soil and her skin is shiny with sweat. She sees me watching her and she smiles and, just for a second, she looks like Mum.

Jim comes over with a big bottle of water and we all stop for a rest. I get to talk to some of the other people on the dig: a woman called Vanessa with long, floaty hair and a fat man with sticky out ears and a bushy beard. He's called Bob and he nods at everything Raine says. He's wearing a tight green tee shirt with **I dig to dig** printed across the front of his big wobbly belly.

Luke's got crisps from somewhere and we eat them in about two seconds. Then it's back to work.

I go and scrape at the earth next to Vanessa. She's really nice and she's very helpful too.

"What would be the best thing to dig something big out of the ground?" I ask her.

"A pick, I suppose," she tells me, "or a mattock." She picks up a long pole thing with a hook on the end and shows me how to push it into the earth and force out a stone.

I try to lift it but it's even heavier than the pickaxe. There's no way I could get this all the way up to Gull Head on my own. The trowel will have to do; it'll take a long time, that's all.

"Find!" Bob's shouting from the other side of the trench. We all rush over to have a look. Everyone's crowded round, peering at something sticking out of the soil about half-way up the side. I have to squeeze between them all and wriggle to get to the front. It's a bone, long and curved and brown with earth.

Bob's working flat out, clearing the soil away from the bone with a tiny brush.

"Easy does it." Raine pushes through the crowd. She sounds really excited.

But it's only a bone.

Now's a good time for me to borrow that little trowel. I wriggle my way back out through all the legs, and go over to where I left it lying on the ground. Quick as anything, I grab it and start to unzip my rucksack. But there's a shadow and someone's leaning over me.

"It's a good idea not to take other people's things," says Raine in a weird, scary voice. "Hasn't your mother taught you that?"

I drop the trowel fast and fiddle around in my bag, pretending I can't hear her.

"Archaeology tools are expensive," she goes on. "We gather them all up at the end of the day and I lock them in my shed. Just to be on the safe side."

I squint up at Raine, and she waves a key at me, swinging it backwards and forwards like a hypnotist. She gives a little laugh, puts the key in her pocket and walks away.

Bob's bone has got everyone excited. They all move over to his side of the trench and start working there. I carry on scraping away with the trowel just like Raine showed me. Those little black flies are back again; the air is sweltering. My arms feel heavy and my hair keeps flopping over my face. We must have been here for hours. Not much sign of a Roman villa so far.

"I think it's time I got you back," says Jim at last, from the side of the trench.

"You can come again another day," Raine tells me, "you've proved to be a jolly good little digger."

I pull my rucksack onto my shoulder and Jim gives me a hand-up out of the trench.

As we walk back across the field, I'm wondering how I can get into that tool shed.

"I bet you've had enough digging to last you all summer," says Jim, swinging the gate open.

That's what he thinks.

Fifteen

I climb into the truck and stuff my rucksack between my feet. It's stifling in here, and we wind the windows down as fast as we can.

"I can't breathe," I tell Jim. My head is prickling and itching and so, so hot.

"Yeah, they hadn't invented air conditioning when this was made," says Luke, banging the side of the truck.

Jim shoots a look at us as he turns the wheel. "Apologies for the sub-standard transport. You can always walk home, y'know."

We bump along the road with the sun flickering through the trees. A fat bluebottle flies in Jim's window and head-butts the windscreen.

It crawls up the glass, falls and bounces away, making little pinging noises. Up and down. *Ping buzz ping*, over and over again.

Luke elbows me. "Hey, don't go to sleep."

"I'm not," I say, feeling my eyelids close. *Buzz-zz* goes the fly.

We go straight to Rosa's. Mum's there already, sitting at the table next to Bee. There's a stew and a mountain of mashed potatoes but I hardly eat a thing. All I want to do is shut my eyes again.

"Why don't you curl up on the sofa, Effie?" Rosa says.

It's just what I want to do. I lie there and listen to them all finishing their tea. I hear Luke yawning. He gets down from the table and says goodnight, even though it's still really early. I hear Rosa taking Bee upstairs for her bath.

When I wake up, there's a blanket over me and I wriggle out a bit because it's so hot and cramped. Mum and Rosa and Jim are sitting at the table, talking. I'm just getting up – but Mum's got that important sound in her voice.

"It *is* a big deal. I've been on my own for years."

Then comes Rosa's voice: "It can't go on. She needs looking after."

"Effie looks after herself – she looks after *me*!" Mum's almost shouting.

I lie there, quiet as a mouse, with my eyes tight shut. If they know I'm awake they'll stop and I won't find out what's going on.

Rosa starts again: "If we move in with you, there'll always be someone around for her. And I can cook. She's half-starved a lot of the time."

I hear something being poured – wine, I reckon.

Then Jim speaks: "It makes sense, Pen. We're all struggling for money. It's gotta be cheaper to run one house instead of two. And Luke and Effie can get to know each other – it'll be like you and me all over again."

I hold my breath, waiting for Mum's answer.

"Sounds like a good idea," she says at last. "When are you moving in?"

And that's when I know we're all going to live together in Crow House.

"Yay!" I shout, throwing off the blanket and

running over to Mum. I put my arms round her and squeeze and squeeze as hard as I can, nearly knocking the wine glass out of her hand.

"Don't you ever have a proper night's sleep, Effie," says Jim, laughing, "even after all that digging?"

"Don't you know I'm nocturnal?" I tell him.

Sixteen

Luke's hopeless at packing. He stands holding some black bin liners, looking at all his clothes in a heap on the bed.

I sit on the floor of his room, rolling a little red ball to Bee.

"Just do it," I tell him.

"What d'you mean? Half this stuff doesn't fit any more."

"You can sort it out when we get there," I say. "Crow House is massive anyway. You'll have a huge bedroom with loads of space."

"Suppose," he says, and starts piling everything into the black bags. He ties them up and dumps them in the corner. Then he goes over to the window and looks out, kicking one foot, over and over, against the wall.

"What's the matter?" Rosa pokes her head in through the doorway. She's got a pile of towels and stuff in her arms.

Luke doesn't turn round. His trainer keeps bashing the wall *thump, thump*. "It's weird … leaving here." He mumbles the words, like they're hard to get out.

"You don't want to live with us!" I say. I can feel my face going red. It'll be tons better living all together. Why doesn't Luke want to?

"Hey," says Rosa. She comes into the room and sits on the bed, putting the towels down next to her. She keeps her eyes on Luke but I think she's talking to me.

"It is hard to leave a place you love, especially a place where you were born. We've had some great times here, but it is too small for us now. It's time to move on."

Luke doesn't answer.

Rosa looks at me and smiles. "Listen, I think we're getting bogged down with the packing. It's so hot – why don't we take the afternoon off? Effie hasn't been to the other side of the island yet. Let's show her Giants' Hall. We can just make the eleven o'clock boat."

I stand next to Luke on the boat, watching the land get smaller and smaller as we speed away, cutting a white V shape through the dark blue waves. White birds dip and tumble, following the boat.

"They're scavengers," Luke tells me, "always after scraps – the rats of the air." He flashes me a grin and I know that everything's all right again.

It's like a different island. Me and Luke are first off the boat, running up the path alongside the little quay. We go along a lane with high bushes each side. Everywhere is green and jungly with tall, leafy trees and bright flowers, pink and orange, flopping out of the bushes like tongues. It's hard to keep up with Luke and he's just in front of me as we turn a bend, onto a gravel path. There's a building, like an open stable or a barn, with a perfect green lawn in front. It's so quiet here; I can hear the silence thumping in my ears.

"This is it," Luke says, crunching across the gravel and running inside: "Giants' Hall."

Peering into the stable, I can see huge wooden statues, painted ones, from the front of old ships. One's a man holding a cross – he's a monk or something – and there's a wooden lady wearing a golden crown. Next to her is a tiger with his mouth open showing red inside and snarling white fangs, ready to pounce. Behind him are two more women in old-fashioned clothes, painted blue and red, and a man in a black coat with shiny gold buttons. They're all facing into the courtyard, looking at me, with their arms stretched out like they're saying, 'Welcome, Effie.'

I love it all.

Some people come down the crunchy gravel path and break the spell.

"Hey," calls Luke, "come and see my favourite."

I step into the stable. Luke's standing in front of a huge wooden man with a turban on and a black bushy beard. He's like Ali Baba from the Forty Thieves, with a glint in his eye and a smile on his fat, red lips. I can see why Luke likes him.

"He's wicked," I say, and I mean it, really

117

wicked. He could be a pirate or a torturer with a whip.

"Which one do you like best?" Luke asks me. "One of those dancing girls?"

"The tiger," I tell him. I spin round on my heels, looking again at all the figureheads. "Or that one there, the woman in the blue dress with her arms chopped off."

"Yeah." Luke snaps out a laugh. "Think of all the blood. Both arms chopped off in those days. No anaesthetic. Agony!"

He points. "Go on then. Stand next to her and I'll take a photo."

A photograph. I can't remember what to do, it's ages since Mum took my photo.

I go over to the figure and put my arms round the woman's waist. Her wooden body is shiny, warm from the sun. I look up at her broken arms and proud, strong face.

Click goes Luke, on his mobile.

We sit on the grass and eat our picnic. I can hear Mum's and Rosa's mumbling voices on the other side of the hedge. Luke bites into his sandwich and chews slowly, looking out to sea. A fly comes and he brushes it away. His eyes are very clear and blue.

"Don't you want to move to Crow House?" I ask.

"Yeah," he says. "It'll be good. It'll be harder to get out at night, that's all. More people about. You know?"

He takes another bite of his sandwich and stares right into my eyes. He *did* see me the other night.

"Why do you do it – go climbing and stuff?"

I wait. Maybe I shouldn't have asked.

"Because I'm stuck on the island, that's why. You've never lived here all your life; you don't know what it's like." He rolls his sandwich wrapper into a ball and scrunches it up. "Just because I was born here, doesn't mean it's all I want."

"But the island is brilliant!" I tell him. "There's the beach and the sea and …" I run out of words. How can he not know?

"Yeah. And everywhere I go, someone remembers me from when I was a little kid. And everything I do, Mum gets to hear about it."

I feel myself going red.

"But that's good, isn't it? Safe," I say.

"You don't get it." He rolls over on the grass, away from me.

I want to know more. "So how does climbing at night help?"

He sits up and hugs his knees. "It's not just climbing, is it? You saw us. It's about being free – like an animal, a bird."

I want to understand, but I don't, not really.

"Anyway," Luke says, "how come you can't swim?"

"Who knows?" It comes out too loud. I think of swimming lessons at my last school, of girls laughing and pointing, of me just standing on the steps. "I don't care, anyway. I hate swimming."

"OK, OK, calm down," Luke says. "But you'd better learn. If you live on an island, you have to know how to swim."

Seventeen

This time, the digging place is exactly as I left it. I haven't got a trowel, like I'd planned – this old spoon will have to do again. I've got my toothbrush in the pocket of my jeans, for scrubbing at all the tricky bits.

I get to work, digging and scraping, burrowing down. All that stuff Raine told me about archaeologists being careful and taking time is very useful, except I get so excited when I'm here, I go faster and faster. Imagine Raine's face when she sees my treasure. And Mum won't have to work at that stinky pub ever again.

The sea's steady today: *whoosh – ahh – whoosh – ahh*, those big steady breaths. The wind lifts my hair and flings it round my head. My lips are salty and dry.

The hole's just big enough for me to squeeze in now and, slipping down the side of the rock, in I go. Straightaway the air's different: cold and moist and secret, like the air in the Bone Cave. The tunnel isn't very long – just a deep hole, really, but it slopes downwards. It seems safe enough, although it's very cramped. That nice Bob man would never fit in here. I touch all around with both hands, checking for anything moving. Nothing. Slabs of stone line the sides and the roof. No animal made this.

I get a little bit further in, scuffling along on my knees and elbows, peering into the blackness. I can't hear the sea or the wind at all now, just the sound of my breathing and a kind of soft beating in my head. I have no idea what's inside the tunnel. On I go, bit by bit, shuffling and panting. Little pointy stones on the cold floor dig into my knees and elbows.

Just like that, the passage stops. A pile of rocks or something is in the way but it's too dark to see properly. I use both hands to scrabble at the stones. They wobble a bit but they seem stuck fast. I manage to get the spoon and stick the handle in between them, though they're stubborn as donkeys. But I'm stubborner.

A scatter of cold soil patters down on my hair and into the back of my tee shirt.

My heart thumps. In my mind comes Raine's clear voice talking about safety helmets – and my head feels very soft and bare. I'm getting out. Now.

Slowly and carefully I back up. I can hear the wind again – and the sea. The sunlight is dazzling as I lean backwards out of the hole and take some deep, clean breaths. I'm covered in soil and muck, all over my hands and arms, down inside my tee shirt and in my hair. My trainers are filthy.

I rest for a bit, thinking. What's hidden in there has got to be really precious, so precious that someone would block it up.

Slowly and carefully I put all the soil and stuff back, using the spoon to scoop and press it into place next to the big rock. It's taking ages. The wind has died down now and the sea sounds calmer. Faraway voices float up to me from the beach.

Something hits against the spoon, flicks up and lands on the grass. I reach over to pick it up: a single golden coin, half-covered with earth. It's not any coin I know. I hold it carefully in my mucky fingers and peer at the decoration – of a tiny horse with its front hooves raised. It looks just like it's dancing.

Eighteen

I'm wild with excitement. The coin is a sign – it must be; a sign that I'm getting close to the treasure chest at last. I want to tell Luke really, really badly, but I want to keep it secret too. I hide the coin deep in my jeans' pocket. At tea, it's like it's burning a hole to get out. I push my hand inside, checking it's safe, feeling its blobby shape with the tips of my finger and thumb.

"What're you wriggling about for?" Luke asks. "Got nits or something?"

I just ignore him.

It takes two days to move the furniture and clothes up to Crow House and everybody's got jobs to do. Luke was right; it is much harder to sneak out now we're all living together. On Monday evening, we're all sitting round the kitchen table with a big meaty smell coming from the stove.

"We'll paint some walls tomorrow," says Rosa, getting up to check on the food. "What colour shall we have the kitchen? Yellow?"

"Yellow?" I say. "I hate yellow."

"How can you hate yellow?"

"Easy. It's the colour of bananas and dandelions and pale, lumpy custard like in the school canteen," I say. "They're all horrible."

"It's the colour of sunshine – of summer – butter – buttercups – and fat, buttery bees!" Rosa twirls round the room, a wooden spoon in her hand, every so often poking it into the bubbling pot of tomatoey stuff that's puffing out steam from the top of the cooker. "Yellow is yum-yum-yummy!" She puts her face close up to Bee in the highchair.

"Yummy! YUMMY!" Bee joins in, banging her spoon on the little table in front of her.

"What colour are you going to paint your bedroom, Effie?" Rosa dips the spoon into the sauce and tastes it.

"Can I paint it?" I ask.

"Of course. What colour was your old room?"

I think of my bedroom at Ellsmere Flats but I can't remember any colour, just the black freckles of damp in the corners.

"Never mind," Rosa says, "we'll go and buy some paint first thing in the morning, right before breakfast. Paint doesn't cost much. One coat should do it."

Rosa's smile is catching and I grin back.

We go to the supermarket in Peterstown for the paint. Rosa whizzes the van into the car park and pulls on the brake right outside the doors.

Inside are massive towers of paint, each tin with a label that shows its colour. They're all in rows with other tins lined up behind them, a silent rainbow army.

"Ooh! Look at that red! Oh, that green is nice. How about green? Or purple?" Rosa lifts up one tin after another, turning each one round and round in her hands before putting it back.

"Stay here and decide – I'll go and get the yellow for the kitchen, and some new brushes."

I don't know how I'll ever choose. I walk up

and down the rows, thinking of my bedroom with the sea outside the window, trying to picture myself looking at a pink wall – or a deep red one. What if I get it wrong? I feel tiny against the towers of paint, trying to make up my mind. Then I see the blue and I know. It's the colour of sky very early in the morning before the weather has made up its mind what to do – a sort of hopeful colour.

I put out my hand to the tin. "That one," I say, when Rosa comes back.

"Ahh," she breathes. "Perfect. I think I've got some curtains to match."

When we get back to Crow House, Bee is crying and Luke's walking about the kitchen jiggling her on his shoulder. Her cheeks are blotchy and red. When she sees Rosa, she screams even louder and holds out her arms. Rosa drops the carrier bags of paint things on the table and scoops Bee into her arms.

I stand in the doorway watching the three of them, with the tin of paint next to me on the floor.

Mum's still asleep when Rosa, Luke and me clear away the breakfast things and get out the paint brushes and rollers. Jim's out on the boat and then at the dig, and Mrs Bowton from the shop is looking after Bee for the day.

"Let's do my room first!" I say.

I want to get back to Gull Head.

"Oh, all right," Rosa tells me. "I wanted to start with the kitchen – but I suppose it doesn't matter which way round we do things."

We have to move my bed out of my room so we push it onto the landing, along with the little table and chair. We pile all my clothes up on the bed and I make sure the treasure is hidden safe in my pillowcase. The golden coin is still in the pocket of my jeans, pushed right to the very bottom.

Luke drags the stepladder in for reaching the high bits. Rosa does the edges with a paintbrush and Luke and I have a roller each. We start near the window next to my bed. It's hard work and soon my arms are aching but Luke and Rosa are really fast.

"How do you get it so smooth?" I ask them.

Luke laughs. "We've done it loads of times

before, haven't we, Mum? For old Mrs Patterson and in our house."

By lunchtime we've finished and we all stand back to look at it. Some parts are wet and dark but the bit around the window and next to my bed is nearly dry.

It is as blue as the sky.

"OK if I go out and see Joe now?" says Luke, rubbing his painty hands on his jeans.

Now's my chance to get away. "I'll look for Shadow outside." I make for the hallway.

"Oh no you don't," Rosa tells us, "you're not slipping off that easily. Stay and help today, then you can both do what you like tomorrow. I want to get started on the kitchen now."

Luke grumbles a bit but we drag the stepladder out of my bedroom and bump it down the stairs.

We sit at the table in the kitchen and eat some cheese and apples with the crusty bread that Rosa gets from the proper baker's. Mum comes in. She's got the big old shirt on with all the splodges of paint down the front – her working shirt.

"Effie," she says, "let's paint a picture on your wall – would you like that? Something to do with the island, maybe. Waves, shells – all along the wall next to your bed."

It's an amazing idea. Mum is an amazing painter. "Yes, let's do it now," I say, getting up and rushing over to her. "Can you do the boats – and the seagulls – and Crow House and the beach – and everything …?"

"The whole of the island on one wall!"

"Only some of it, the best bits. Can you? Please." I put my arms round her waist and start pushing her towards the door.

She's got that faraway look in her eyes, as if she's deep in her painting already, as if I'm not really here.

I carry on pushing.

"But what about the kitchen? Have Luke and I got to do it all by ourselves?" says Rosa. She's smiling, though, so I know it's OK.

The wall near my bed is already dry. Mum gets her box of paints and we choose the blues, greens, greys and pinks for the picture, just Mum and me. She gets out her fat black pencil and, kneeling down on the floor, carefully does the outline of all the shapes right onto my wall. She does the beach in front, with shells and seaweed and rocks. And she sketches the sea behind with one bobbing fishing boat. In the distance is Crow House, high on top of the hill. She has to stand up to do that part.

We step back and check that all the bits are pencilled in.

"I'll start with the close-ups, today," she tells me. "Why don't you get me some water to rinse my brush in?"

I fetch some water from the bathroom and, when I get back, Mum's started on a shell, one of those pinky-white ones with tiny grey stripes. It looks so real, the way she's done it, that I think I could pick it up.

"You could paint some of the seaweed," Mum tells me, as I carefully put the tooth mug full of water down next to her.

I mix up some of the green and add a bit of red to get the brown colour.

"It's scary painting onto a wall," I say.

"Go on, have a try," Mum says. "I can always go over it." She gives me one of her tiny artist's brushes.

I dip it in the paint and touch the very tip of the brush to the wall. There it is, my first lump of seaweed.

We paint for ages. In the end my knees are sore from kneeling and I need a wee, but Mum just carries on.

I go to the bathroom, then I run downstairs to see Rosa and Luke.

The kitchen is half-done in yellow paint. Luke's up the ladder, doing the top near the ceiling, and Rosa is finishing the wall near the window.

"What do you think, Effie?" she asks.

"I love it," I say. It looks like the sun is shining, even though it's grey outside.

"What about bananas and lumpy custard?" Luke says, turning round from the top of the ladder.

"They are a completely different colour," I tell him.

"We won't finish today," Rosa says. "Jim will be home soon from the dig, and starving hungry I expect, and Bee's due back at six."

I have a drink of water from the tap, and run back upstairs to my room.

At the doorway I stop: the painting is wonderful. While I've been downstairs, Mum's made it look like all the shells and rocks and seaweed are wet and shiny; a real, live beach on my bedroom wall. And in the middle of all the shells and weed is something else – round, conker-brown, with a hole in the middle. It's a sea-bead. Amazing.

Mum's sitting on the floor looking up at me. "I know how much you want one," she says.

I feel a flutter inside.

"Thank you. This is the best bedroom in the world," I tell her.

My room is suddenly full of people. Rosa and Luke come in, and Rosa's got Bee in her arms, and they're saying what a brilliant artist Mum is, and aren't I lucky. And I think maybe they're right.

Nineteen

I'm in bed with all my clothes on. I lie straight and still under the duvet, waiting. There's no way I'm going up to Gull Head in the middle of the night – but I am tracking Luke. The sea is quiet tonight, the waves rolling slowly in and out, like someone breathing. I can hear the adults talking downstairs in the kitchen – that's Rosa, high and rushing, and Jim, low and steady. Mum's laugh comes every now and then, short and loud.

Rosa and Jim come upstairs first. I hear them moving past my door, whispering. Jim says something and laughs.

"Shh." Rosa giggles. "You'll wake the children."

They go on along the hallway and their door closes with a *snick*.

For a little while, Mum's on her own downstairs. She plays a sad, sad song on Jim's guitar, the same little part over and over:

"I saw the new moon dah-dah-dah …"

I hear the downstairs lights go off – *click, click* – and she creaks up the stairs to her bed.

When all the bathroom taps have stopped running, and everything's silent, Luke moves. He pads along the hall and I hear the stairs groan.

I'm up and out of my bedroom in a flash. I slip down the stairs after him, pulling on my fleece. At the back door, I push my feet in my trainers and hurry down the path.

It's warm and still outside, with a big white moon. The bushes rustle and sway as I brush past them. I get to the top of the hill and see Luke already on his way down.

I race after him.

As I go, I pick up speed. Soon I'm running so hard my heart hammers and my throat burns. But I must keep him in sight. Luke doesn't go along the quay tonight; he turns right along the

136

seafront and heads across the top of the beach towards White Rocks and the long curve of silvery sea. The rocks stand at the top of the beach with a concrete path and a wall behind them. Luke's a tiny figure lit by the moon against the huge, dark sky. He's nearly at the rocks now, and others are coming too, from all directions. I count eight figures, running and leaping.

I keep my eyes on Luke and run towards him. When I reach him, I'm panting.

I say his name. Everyone stops moving.

"Did Mum wake up?" Luke asks.

I shake my head.

The other boys are silent – waiting.

"Show me how to do it," I say to Luke. "Show me the right way."

"There is no right way," says one boy.

A big boy with long hair walks over. "Just run," he tells me. "Run up to that rock and climb to the top."

He's pointing at a massive rock with really steep sides.

I feel everyone looking at me. My heart is banging. I'll show them; I'll do it.

I run up to the rock and put one foot up as

high as I can.

I fall back.

The boy with long hair sniggers.

I wish I'd never come.

Then Luke steps forward. "Do it at your own speed," he says. "This time, don't look at the rock. See yourself on the other side."

I try to do what he says. I feel everyone watching me as I take a long run-up. I get to the wall and I'm fine, and I'm going up it – nearly to the top – but I can't do it.

I fall again, twisting over on my ankle.

The boys slowly move away. They clamber over the rocks, spinning and somersaulting.

But Luke's still next to me. "Hey, you were almost there," he says. "Then you thought too much and made yourself afraid." His eyes are shining in the moonlight. "Why not just get the feel of the wall for now? Do some flips against it, stuff like that?"

He runs at the wall, putting one arm forward, touching it, kicking it, spinning away.

I do the same. I run against it, feeling the knobbly concrete against my hand, twisting my body, flipping round, and away. I do it again and again, and I get higher and higher.

"Yeah," shouts Luke, "that's it. It's not a competition – just enjoy it, just keep moving."

I run and jump and spin, over and over, not thinking, just moving. And I'm going higher and higher each time. I'm climbing the wall.

At last I'm tired. I want to be back at Crow House, in my bed. Some of the boys have gone already. Yawning, I watch Luke run along the top of the wall and spring off. He lands next to me, puffing a bit.

"Time to go?" he asks.

We walk back along the sand with Luke's friend Tom. The sea is dark and shiny, with the tiny lights of fishing boats bobbing up and down. Hanging in the sky above us is the moon, huge and ghost-white.

At the end of the beach, Tom goes straight on towards the town and Luke and me head home.

"Feeling good?" Luke asks.

"Yes," I say, and I am. My body's tired but my head is wide awake. Is this what it's like to be an animal?

"Yeah. Free-running makes you feel like that. Like you can do anything."

He turns back to face me and I can see his wide smile.

"Aren't you ever scared of falling?" I ask.

"Don't think about it. Just move," he says.

We're both quiet, walking slowly up the hill.

"When I'm older, I'll learn circus skills. Live on the mainland for a bit," Luke says.

I grit my teeth. I don't want him to go away.

"What about you?"

"I'm going to make a fortune," I say.

Back in my bedroom I open my curtains, letting in the cold moonglow. I take the brooch from under my pillow and follow the curves of the eagle's feathers with my finger. With my hand closed tight around the brooch, I shut my eyes, wishing hard.

Twenty

I sit up in bed with early morning light streaming in through the window. There's a whispery, panting noise coming from over in the corner. I push the brooch to safety and wriggle to the bottom of the bed to look. It's Shadow. He's in the corner of the room in a pile of my clothes, turning round and round, pulling at the clothes with his claws.

He wails, thin and high, like he's hurt.

I go over to him and see his sides heaving in and out. His eyes are wide open, staring into nothing.

He's dying right in front of me.

I get as near as I dare but I'm scared to touch

him. What can I do? I can feel a big sob coming up from inside me.

Shadow's breathing louder and louder. His sides are moving and jumping about, he must be in pain, poisoned. There's something coming out of his bum, something dark and wet and spreading. Blood.

Oh, god! I'll get Rosa. Don't die, Shadow. Please don't die.

I'm getting up to fetch Rosa when I see it. A brownish lump slithers from between Shadow's legs. I can see four little legs all folded up, and the tiny, blind face of a kitten, pressed against the inside of a kind of slippery bubble. It's like looking through soft, slimy plastic. A kitten, covered in dark stuff, like feathers. Shadow's licking and licking at it, and the feathers turn to fur: black, wet fur.

"You clever, clever thing." I keep on saying it, over and over.

The kitten's wriggling and squirming about, making tiny, squeaky mews. Shadow's sides are still moving and right then two more kittens slide out.

They all lie wriggling in their nest of clothes,

and I watch Shadow licking and licking her brand-new family. And Shadow – who's a SHE but we never knew it – starts purring her head off.

It takes nearly all day to sort out the kittens. Rosa says I can't keep them in my bedroom because of the fleas, so Luke and me run to the corner shop and ask Mrs Bowton for a big cardboard box, to make a bed.

"We need something soft to put in the bottom for them," says Rosa. "How about that old pink cardigan of yours, Penny?"

"My favourite cardi!" says Mum, but she's laughing. "It's about time I got rid of that thing."

I put it in the box and we bring all the cats downstairs to their new home.

Jim's late back; Bee's already in bed and Luke's gone round to Tom's.

Jim kicks his boots off at the door and comes into the kitchen. He's got mud up both arms and all down his tee shirt. And his face looks awful, like he's got the flu or something.

"Whatever's the matter?" Rosa asks. She gets up and goes over to him.

"Not now," he says. "I'm going for a bath."

Without saying anything to us, he walks through the kitchen and goes upstairs. But I see him look right in Rosa's face and I know something bad has happened.

I sit at the table, quiet as anything, waiting to hear what it is.

"Well?" asks Rosa, when Jim's had his bath and is just about to eat. "Tell us about it."

"Later," he says.

It's obvious I'm going to have to go upstairs before he'll say anything interesting. I start yawning and stretching a bit.

"You look tired, Effie," says Rosa. "Why don't you go up to bed early? That lovely blue room is waiting for you."

"Night," says Mum, picking up Jim's guitar.

And off I go, out of the kitchen and up the stairs.

I get into my pyjamas as fast as I can, and tiptoe back to the top of the staircase. All I can hear is a jumble of voices through the open kitchen door. I creep back down the stairs, keeping to the wall, like a detective on telly.

I walk as quietly as I can back down the hallway and stand behind the door to the kitchen.

Now no one's saying anything.

At last I hear a chair scraping back along the floor. Through the gap between the door and doorframe, I can just see half of Mum with her hands resting on the table. She's turning her glass of wine round and round. They've got the back door open, and little puffs of wind blow in and ruffle up her hair.

"Well, any other ideas?" It's Rosa and she sounds worried.

"We'll have to go back to the mainland. I'll take Effie and we'll try to get our old flat back. There's no point staying here, with nowhere to live," says Mum.

What does she mean, nowhere to live? What about Crow House? I've missed something really, really important. I jiggle up and down, waiting for someone else to speak: why won't they *hurry up*?

"Penny, you can't leave now," says Jim. "You've promised Effie."

"Don't make me feel worse." Mum drinks the whole of her glass in one big gulp and fills it up again from the green bottle on the table. "Raine never backs down. If she wants to chuck us all out on the streets, she will." Her voice is wobbly. "I've spent years trying to stand up to her – she always wins in the end."

"I can't believe she'd do it." It's Rosa's voice. "She knows we've just given up the other house. There's nothing else on the island, not that we can afford. We'll ask her to think again."

I don't want to hear any more. I run back down the hallway and up the stairs to my room and throw myself down on my bed. I'm shaking and cold as ice, even though it's so hot. Through the window I can see the moon's ghost face in the purple sky. I stare at Mum's half-finished painting on the wall, and the tears start to come, but I crunch my teeth together to stop them.

It's a long time before Luke gets home. I hear him pad across the landing and go into his bedroom.

I'm up and in his room as quick as anything,

closing the door behind me. He's over near the window, pulling off his tee shirt.

"What's going on?" he asks.

"Raine's throwing us out. All of us. I heard them talking. We've got to stop it, otherwise we'll be split up and Mum and I'll have to go back to the mainland and I'll never see you or Rosa or Bee for years and years – and oh, it's all HORRIBLE." The words come out in a jumble and I really am crying now.

Luke just stands there, staring.

"What are you on about?" he says. "We've only just moved here. Have you had a nightmare or something?"

"Of course not! I went down and listened. Jim's in a funny mood – ever since he came in he's been grumpy – I knew something was going on. They've all been talking about it."

"Prob'ly not definite." Luke stretches and yawns. "There's nothing we can do now, anyway. Go to sleep, Effie. Things'll be OK."

"They won't, you'll see. Don't say I didn't warn you."

I stomp off, back to my own room, and let the door bang behind me.

Next minute, Rosa's peeping in through my door. "Effie, are you still awake?" she whispers.

But I just lie still until she goes away. I lie watching the moon through the window and all the billions of twinkling stars. I'm full of plans, swirling round and round in my head.

Raine wouldn't really chuck us out, would she? Just now I've started to trust her?

The next morning they tell us.

We're all at the kitchen table and Bee is banging her spoon on her green plastic mug. "Dah-dah-dah," she goes.

Mum comes in, in her old flowery pyjamas, and sits down next to me.

"We've got some bad news," Rosa says.

Jim pours some more coffee from the jug on the table.

They're waiting for us to ask questions. I make a face at Luke but he's not looking.

"What?" I ask.

"You know already, don't you?" says Mum, giving me a funny look. "Did you listen to us talking last night?"

Then I'm mad as anything. "Yeah, I did, 'cause it's the only way I get to find out what's going on. You're running away again and we're going to leave this place – Crow House and the island – and I'll never forgive you!"

Mum doesn't say a word.

"It's not your mum's fault," says Jim. "The dig isn't going well. Raine's not finding what she wanted – and her money's been stopped. It means she'll have to go and work somewhere else."

"So what?" says Luke. "Why does that mean *we* have to go anywhere?"

"You know that Crow House belongs to her," says Rosa, "and it costs such a lot to keep going with such a big garden and everything. We can ask her to think again – but if she's selling it, there's nothing much we can do."

"We can buy it," I say.

They all stare at me – and it's complete silence. Even Bee stops banging and dah-ing. And I'm going to tell them, about the brooch and the bracelet and everything – but Jim starts laughing. He rocks back on his chair and he's laughing away like crazy.

"Yeah, let's *buy* it, everyone! Now why didn't we think of that?"

"Oh, Effie, if only we could –" Rosa starts, but I'm off out the door and scooting down the garden path.

It's so hot today, like the air is a big blanket pressing down on me, making it hard to breathe. I climb the cliff path and I have to keep stopping because I'm puffed out. There's no breeze at all. Those tiny black flies are back again, buzzing round my head worse than ever.

By the time I get to Gull Head, I'm so sweaty and tired, I don't feel much like digging and today I don't even have the spoon – but I've got to do something.

There's no one about, as usual, except the fierce old gulls, diving and screaming in the sky. I heave the stone away from the hole. I lie flat out on the springy heather and start to dig. The earth near the top is dry and crumbly in my fingers, and the smell of dark, rich soil comes up as I burrow down. I go deeper, scrabbling with my hands and scraping with my nails, all the time keeping a lookout for coins. Maybe it was just one that dropped out as people dragged the treasure chest into the passage?

There's a whistle, loud and long. It's a man on the cliff path, looking right at me.

"Here, Bingo!" he shouts.

A little white dog is pelting across the grass towards me. I'm scrabbling at the earth, as fast as I can, trying to cover up my digging, pulling the boulder back over the hole. But the dog's here now, panting, snuffling, yapping his head off *Yip-Yip*. He's dancing about on top of my digging place, scuffing up the ground with his short legs. As fast as I push the earth back, the dog digs it out again, like it's a game. Bits of earth, roots and grass shower around us. And the gulls are going crazy, screaming and swooping low over my head.

"BINGO!" shouts the man again, marching over. He's waving a dog lead about and he's red and sweaty-looking.

Bingo carries on; he's got his head and his two front paws down inside my hole now, sending out earth between his back legs. His little tail is wagging like mad.

The man leans forward and grabs Bingo's collar, fixing on the lead and yanking him out. "I am sorry," he says to me. "I don't know what's got into him – rabbits, I suppose. He fair tore this spot up a few days ago, before I could stop him."

I smile up at the man, hoping he'll go away. Bingo's yapping and yapping, pulling on his lead – frantic – his two front legs paddling in the air. He wants to get back in the hole.

"Have you lost something?" the man asks.

I stare at him like I don't know what he's going on about.

"I saw you digging," he explains, bending over, peering around at the grass and heather.

"Beetles," I say, quick as I can, my face burning red. "For school."

For a second, I don't think he believes me. Bingo makes a high whiny howl.

"Ah, Natural History Project, eh?" The man straightens up again. "Good luck, then. Come along, Bingo." He pulls Bingo away, back to the path. "We'll come and see what you've found on our way back from our walk."

I pretend to start searching in the ground

again, watching them through my hair until they're just tiny dots.

I'd better cover this up again for now, in case they do come back.

I definitely won't be able to keep this place secret for much longer.

Twenty-one

There's no one in when I get home. I go to the sink for some water and swallow it down in great gulps. Shadow climbs out of the box under the window and rubs against me, saying hello. All the time, the kittens squeak and peep, calling her back to them.

I curl up in the armchair. Crow House is silent, except for the kittens making licking and sucking noises from their bed in the corner. There's no way I can get the chest up without proper digging tools. Somehow, I'll have to get into Raine's shed.

The door swings open and it's Luke. He throws a fishy-smelling parcel down on the table.

"Where did you get to? Mum's really worried." He goes over to the kitten-box and crouches down, stroking the cats. Shadow goes mad, purring at his fishy hands. I lean forward to watch her turning round and round in the box, licking him and rubbing her whiskery face against his arm. Luke talks with his back to me. "About this morning – they're all really sorry. Especially Jim. For laughing – you know?"

I want to tell him about the treasure. Soon, but not yet.

"Will you come with me to Raine's? I don't know the way," I say instead.

"Raine's? It's miles away – and it's baking out." Luke leaves the kittens and throws himself into a chair at the table. He pulls off his wellies. "No. I'm not going over there, I don't want to see her." He kicks his boots across the floor.

Shall I tell him? I open my mouth ready to begin – and close it again.

It's like I've got to keep it secret just a little bit longer.

"Tell me the way then," I ask. "Show me on a map or something – and write down the address. It's important. Please."

"It's miles. It'll take you ages. Do you want to have another fight with her? It won't do any good, you know. Mum's gone to see Mr Eldridge about getting us somewhere else to live."

Luke stands up and goes over to the sink to wash his hands. He squirts loads of washing-up liquid into the bowl and runs the tap hard.

I go upstairs to my bedroom and take out my treasure. I sit on the floor on my heels and carefully lift the heavy bracelet thing onto my lap. Little specks of earth are still caught in the twists of metal but it's real gold, that's for sure, though it's far too big to go round anyone's arm. Sunlight streams in through the window, making the eagle eyes burn red like fire.

In all the films I've seen, the treasure chests have heaps of golden coins and jewels in them, not brooches and things like this.

My golden coin is still safe in the pocket of my jeans.

I hear Luke come upstairs and go into his room. He's got a football in there, and he kicks it *boof, boof* against the wall, over and over again.

The sun's making a pattern of light across the floor and the painting Mum's done next to my bed is all yellowy-golden. This is the best place I've ever lived. I sit on my bed and hold the bracelet in my lap, thinking.

"Why d'you want to go to Raine's, anyway?" Luke's leaning on the side of the door, looking in.

I shove the bracelet and the brooch behind me.

Luke comes and kneels on my bed with the football under his arm. The fishiness has all gone and he smells of Luke again.

Suddenly I want to tell him.

"Luke, I know how we can save Crow House."

He sighs.

"Effie. There's nothing –"

"Close your eyes," I tell him. "Just close your eyes a minute and hold out your hands. Don't look until I tell you."

Luke shuts his eyes and shuffles nearer to me on the bed. He holds out his hands, like he's getting a present.

I reach for the brooch. I put the bracelet carefully into his open hands. I hold my own hand out flat, with the brooch on it.

"OK," I say. "You can look now."

Luke opens his eyes. He stares at the things. His eyes get wider and wider.

"Are they yours?" he asks, looking up, his blue eyes staring right into mine.

"Aren't they brilliant? I found them, up on Gull Head. And there's more down there – a whole load of treasure."

"But Effie, this stuff is … real. I mean, it's worth loads. I think."

He's twisting and turning the bracelet slowly, round and round.

"Exactly. I'm going to get the rest of the treasure up. Then we can sell it and buy Crow House from Raine and she'll never be able to chuck us out. But first we've got to get hold of some proper digging tools. I know they're in Raine's shed …"

I stop. Luke is looking at me like I'm talking rubbish.

"What?" I say.

"This stuff, it's got to be tested first, to see if it really is old – or just fake. And if it is real, it needs to be put in a museum. We have to hand it in." He says it very slowly and clearly, like I'm deaf, like I'm a baby.

I snatch the bracelet back. "There's no way I'm handing it in! I wish I hadn't told you now."

I push the brooch and the bracelet into my pillowcase and ram it under my bed. I can't believe Luke. I can't believe him. But he just sits there, staring at me.

"Let's tell Jim," he says. "He'll know what to do. You found it, but it belongs to the farmer, Effie. Maybe, if it is treasure, there might be a way for us to get a reward?"

I stand right in front of him and say in my loudest voice, "We aren't telling anyone. OK? It's *my* brooch and *my* bracelet."

The football rolls to the edge of the bed and bounces onto the floor. It rolls away across the floorboards. That's the only sound in all the silence of my room.

Luke's still looking at me.

"It's a torc," he says, very quietly.

I don't know what he's talking about.

"It's not a bracelet. It's a torc. They wore them in the Iron Age and Ancient Rome – around their necks. Only kings and queens had them, I think."

My heart starts to flutter.

"*Are* you going to help me?" I ask.

Luke nods his head, just a bit.

"YAY!"

I pull out the golden coin from my pocket and put it between my teeth. I bite down on it hard, just like they do in the movies.

Twenty-two

I'm starving so we make some sandwiches before we go.

"I've never seen anyone eat as much as you," Luke tells me. "Especially someone so small."

"Food helps me think," I tell him.

Luke sits next to me on the step to eat the sandwiches. Shadow comes rubbing round us, and we give her a share. The kittens are squeaking and squawking from the box all the time she's away from them.

"They go crazy when their mum's not around," Luke says.

"They want to make sure she knows they're

still there," I say, my mouth full of sandwich. "In case she forgets them."

"What tools do we need?" Luke asks.

"Spades and trowels, I think; anything we can get hold of." I poke my rucksack with my foot. "And some kind of sack to put all the treasure in. Our rucksacks might not hold everything."

Luke laughs, and his eyes crinkle. He's as excited as I am.

"Why don't we just go down to the dig now? It's the last day; we can ask to borrow what we want."

"Raine'll ask too many questions. She's clever."

Luke takes another bite of his sandwich. I watch him chewing and thinking.

Suddenly I want to get going. "Come on. Let's see what happens when we get there. One person distracts her. The other one gets the stuff."

Luke gives me a look. "I'm not stealing anything," he says.

"Neither am I. We'll borrow it, get the treasure up this evening, and put all the tools back tomorrow."

Luke stands up, pulls his backpack down from behind the door and we're off.

When we get to the site, there's hardly anyone about.

Bob is folding up some big sheets of blue plastic. He comes towards us, still folding as he walks. He's wearing the green tee shirt again but there's a rip all down one side and I can see tufts of his hairy belly peeping through. His face is really sad, like he'll burst out crying any minute.

"You've heard the news, I suppose?" he says. "There's no villa after all."

I wish I could tell him about the treasure, to cheer him up. I bet he'd love to help us.

A tall figure comes up behind him.

"Hello Lucas. Hello Effie." Raine smiles that not-really-a-smile.

"Hi," Luke and I say together.

"I'm afraid there's not much going on today. We're abandoning the project."

"We wondered if you'd like any help …?" I ask.

"To pack up …?" finishes Luke.

"You can help me put all the tools in the van, if you like."

It's as easy as that.

Luke and I carry the tools under our arms up to Raine's Land Rover under the trees. I dip down behind the Land Rover and open my rucksack and Luke's bag. I push a pointy trowel in each bag and a shovel in mine. Luke goes down for the next load of tools and comes back dragging two picks. They leave long snaky marks in the soil behind him.

While he goes back to help Raine with the last lot of stuff, I heave one of the picks into the Land Rover. I shove the other pick into Luke's backpack, on top of the trowel. The pick's really heavy and hard to get in. The sharp ends keep getting stuck in the sides. I'm getting all hot.

"Are you having a problem?" Bob's right next to me. I don't know how long he's been there. Has he seen me taking the things?

I watch his eyes go from my red face to my rucksack. It's still open and the trowel is poking out of the top, clear as anything.

"I like gardening," I blurt out. It's sort of true. I like gardens, anyway.

I stand there trying to think of something else to say. Anything.

"Jim says they're going to plant potatoes."

"I suppose you want to join in with the grown-ups, eh? You and your cousin, helping. Well, good luck to you all. Here's my archaeology trowel. You can borrow it for a while, as long as it finds its way back to me when you've finished."

Bob puts his trowel into my rucksack and pulls the cord shut.

"Thanks very much," I tell him. I like Bob. I'll make sure he gets a gold coin.

Raine and Luke come up with the last of the things. They pack them into the back of the van. Luke slowly lifts his backpack then drops it down again with a funny look on his face.

Raine turns and stares down onto the mess of earth and bare flat ground left after the dig. She stares and stares. And I see that her eyes are full of tears.

"I was sure I'd found it," she says.

For the first time ever I feel a bit sorry for her.

She pulls open the door of the Land Rover and throws herself inside.

"Goodbye Bob. Thank you for your help. Can

I give you children a lift home?" she asks.

"We'll come back and help put the stuff in your shed for you," Luke tells her, before I can answer.

Clever Luke. Of course we have to do that.

There's no way I'm sitting in the front next to Raine. Luke pulls the seat forward and we both make a scramble for the back. I win and throw my rucksack in first, pretending it's light as a feather.

Scrunched up next to my rucksack and all the plastic sheets, I look at the back of Raine's head. Her white hair is pulled up into a tight knot with little fuzzy bits sticking out at the sides and her neck is red from the sun. She drives slowly over the bumpy field and onto the lane.

It's a really short ride to her house. Eel Cottage looks different this time, not creepy at all. The green stuff hanging down around the door is full of purple flowers.

Raine parks the Land Rover and we climb out. We drop our bags in the hedge at the side of her front path and Raine loads us up with armfuls of tools. She goes round to the back garden and we stumble after her to the shed. It's shut with a big silver lock.

"Stack it all neatly in here, please," says Raine, opening the shed door. "Then come into the kitchen for a drink – and make sure you leave your muddy boots outside."

After putting the tools in the shed, we go into Raine's lemony kitchen for a drink. It's not tea this time, only water. Afterwards, I ask to go upstairs to the bathroom.

"Hurry up," Luke tells me, low, through his teeth.

I go into the hallway with all the paintings and the horns and stuffed animals and climb the stairs. *Tock tock* goes the clock. At the top of the stairs I smell soap and bathroom smells outside one door.

When I've finished, I'm on my way back down when I see another door is open. Raine's bedroom? I'll just have a peep. I walk, soft as I can, across the landing and slip inside the room. There's a giant bed with a white cover and huge windows looking out over the fields and the sea. It's hot and scenty. I go across the soft white carpet towards the light. Right below me, Luke's sitting in the garden poking about with a stick. I turn back into the room.

Against one wall are two cupboards with a big mirror on top. In front of the mirror is a spiky hairbrush, some pots and jars, make-up probably, and a box. Hanging from the mirror is Raine's necklace of shiny sea-beads. I go slowly across and pick up the hairbrush. Caught in its spikes are two long white hairs.

The wooden box is just like the one Mum's got, where she keeps those old letters and the photo of my dad, with the exact same picture of a moon on the lid, made out of that stuff from seashells.

I can't stop myself. I open the lid of Raine's box and there's the same ballet dancer with the two little mirrors behind her. Slowly, slowly, she turns round and round, and the clockwork tune plays each note:

"*I – saw – the – new – moon –*" over and over again.

In front of the dancer are two drawers with silk tassels. I pull out one of the drawers and look at Raine's secret things. There's a real dried rose, faded brown. Next to it is a strip of paper. I take it out carefully with the tips of my fingers – a little paper bracelet with the words PENELOPE INNIS written on it: Mum's name.

I put back the bracelet and pull open the other drawer. In a kind of little net thing there's something curled up, something soft. Slowly I pick it up. It's silky and light, springing out of the net and onto my hands – it's hair; long golden strands.

I curl it into the net again, put it back in the drawer and close the lid with a soft click.

I look up. In the mirror it's the White Witch; she's standing right behind me, watching.

I'm off.

Diving past Raine, down the stairs I go, two at a time, racing through the hallway, out through the kitchen, snatching up my trainers – straight past Luke and into the bright afternoon. The salty smell of the sea hits me. Horrible gulping sounds are bursting up from my insides – I'm scared and giggling, both together. Luke's saying something but I have to get away. I grab my rucksack and drag it out onto the lane.

"What?" Luke's asking, pulling his own rucksack onto one shoulder. "What's up?"

"She caught me. Raine caught me." It's all I can say.

"Yeah, you were ages … she went upstairs. Big deal. It's not like you're a burglar or anything. She's your gran."

All the way home, Luke and me have to keep stopping for a rest.

"Do we really need all these tools, Effie?" he moans, thumping his rucksack down on the ground for the hundredth time and rubbing his shoulder. We're in a lane, leaning on a farmer's gate, two fields away from Crow House.

"It's better to have too many," I say, "then we can definitely get the treasure up tonight. I'm not going back to Raine's again."

"What spooked you, back there?" he asks, climbing on the gate and hanging over, into the field. "Why'd you run out like that? Bones in the bathroom? Skulls in the sink? Skeletons in the –"

"Shut up." I tell him about the paper bracelet and the golden hair. "Do you think it's my mum's hair?"

"Duh. Of course," he says. "From when she was just a kid."

"But Raine was horrible to Mum. That's why she ran away. Why would she keep her things?"

"Search me," Luke says, balancing on the gate with one foot, "she's not my grandmother. But it's the sort of thing my mum'd do. She's got a curl of my hair from when I was a baby."

And for the second time in my life I feel sorry for Raine. Maybe she never meant to be so bossy? I think Rosa is right. I think we should give Raine a second chance – but I'm still getting the treasure, just in case.

From far away there comes a long roll of thunder.

"Hey," Luke says, jumping down, "we'd better get a move on. They've forecast a storm."

Twenty-three

We get to the top of the path near Crow House and I am the tiredest ever. I'm the hottest of hot too. My face is burning and my head is pricking with sweat. My rucksack feels like there's a million stones inside. I know Luke must feel the same; his rucksack is tons heavier than mine.

"This'd better be worth it," he grumbles again.

The thunder is booming overhead now and the sky is really dark, like night. There's a massive *crack!* Over on the headland, a zigzag of lightning spears down into the sea.

The rain starts to fall just as we turn in through the gate. Fat, cold splats of rain come crashing down, faster and faster, pelting me on my head and shoulders. I can hardly see in front of me. Another *crack!* and the sky lights up with a big white Z. It's so loud and huge, like ancient gods fighting – but exciting too. Me and Luke are both skidding on the grass now, ducking under the trees round the side of the house, and slipping on the stony bit under the window. We fall in the door just as another *boom* sounds overhead.

The smell of cooking hits me and my stomach leaps. I'm shivering and shaking. Rosa comes at us with a big towel each. We drop our bags on the floor near the wellies and kick off our trainers. My jeans are black with rain and my teeth are chattering.

"Thank goodness you're back!" Rosa says, rubbing Luke's head with a big pink towel. She rubs my head too, so hard it makes my ears burn.

I'm glad to be home.

Mum's over near the window, watching us, plucking at the strings of Jim's guitar. "Two little drowned rats," she says.

"Get those wet things off," Rosa tells us. "Go up now, both of you, and jump in the bath.

Quickly. Five minutes each. Effie, you go first."

I dash through the hallway with the towel over my head – and bang straight into Raine.

"Hello again, Effie," she says.

Her face is fierce: she knows.

My heart does a double-thump. I squeak, "Hello," and race past her up the stairs.

I grab some clean clothes from my room and have the quickest bath ever. When I come out of the bathroom, I pass Luke on the landing. He's shivering in his towel and his hair is sticking up in tufts all over his head.

"Raine knows we've got the stuff," I whisper.

"Don't worry about it," he says, dodging into the steamy bathroom.

I hang about until Luke is ready, then we go back downstairs. Raine's over by the window now and Mum's standing next to her. It's still raining hard outside, I can hear it hammering on the glass.

Everyone's standing up so Luke and me stand too. It's just like being in Miss Nungent's office for talking in tests.

"You might be wondering why I'm here?" says Raine in that snaky voice of hers, that tells me she's building up to something. She's glaring at me too.

There's this big silence. I can feel Luke next to me, jiggling his hand in the pocket of his jeans.

"I'm here," Raine goes on, "to recover my lost property. I *can* count, you realise."

I remember in all the films about the Right To Remain Silent. It seems like a brilliant idea.

Raine is getting redder and redder and she's all puffed up, like she's going to pop.

"Two archaeological trowels, one brand-new hand shovel and one wooden-handled pick." She says it like a shopping list but all mean and scary. And her eyes are splinters. "Get them now, please."

Me and Luke hurry across to our bags and get out the things. I put the trowels and the shovel down on the kitchen table in front of Raine and Luke drags the pick across and leans it against the table leg. "Sorry," we both mumble.

In one swoop, she bundles all her things into a massive bag on the floor.

She glares at us again. "I think I should report you both to the police for theft."

"That's not fair. We were going to put them

back!" I tell her. I can feel my lip start to wobble.

"Don't you dare answer me back," says Raine.

And I'm so tired and everything's so hard. I haven't really done anything wrong but maybe Luke was right all the time – we should have asked first. My eyes are full of tears and I'm blinking to get them away, but more and more keep coming.

Then Mum's in front of Raine and she's talking in a big, strong voice:

"How DARE you call my daughter a thief. My way is not your way. I haven't made her stick to all the rules you gave us. But she knows right from wrong, and if she says she was only borrowing your tools, then I believe her. Going to the police is ridiculous! She is your granddaughter after all."

No one says anything. There's just the rain hammering down. The window glass is all steamed up, like we've used up all the oxygen with shouting.

Raine is glaring at Mum now, much worse than when she was glaring at me. "Well, that's it then. As a *grandmother* I was going to give you all the time you needed to find somewhere else to live. But from now on, I shall act as a *landlord*."

Raine picks up her bag of tools and marches out the door, into the storm. I hear the Land Rover squeal and roar away. I can't believe it. Just when I was giving her a second chance.

I go over to Mum and put my arms right round her, and she doesn't pull away.

"You were pretty amazing," Luke tells her.

"Like a tiger defending her cub," says Rosa.

Maybe because Mum's so small and skinny and looks nothing like a tiger, we all start laughing. And once we start we can't stop.

All through tea we keep bursting into giggles. When Jim comes home we tell him all about it and he thinks we're crazy.

"If you want to borrow Raine's precious tools you should ask first," he says grumpily. "And what are you going to do when we're all out on the streets? You won't be laughing then."

But I know something no one else does. I've still got Bob's trowel in my rucksack.

Twenty-four

Luke and me go to bed at the same time. I'm so tired, I can feel my eyes drooping. On the way upstairs, we stop and look out through the window. Right across the bay, the storm is still raging. There's no way we're going up to Gull Head tonight.

"D'you know something funny?" says Luke, "No one asked us what we were going to do with Raine's tools."

"Yeah. And something even funnier is, we've still got one trowel left."

I tell him about Bob letting me borrow it.

"So the plan's back on?" Luke says, grinning.

"You bet," I say.

In the morning, it's still raining so hard that no one goes out. The fishing boats are grounded for the day, so it's a kind of holiday for Jim, and Mum doesn't work today anyway.

"There's no point opening the shop," says Rosa. "Only ducks will be out in weather like this and they don't spend money."

We watch the news of flooding on the telly. The reporter says there's been the most rain in one night ever on our island. The pictures show it rushing down the high street like a tsunami.

Luke and me play cards on my bed. Through the window, we can see the waves crashing against the cliffs down at Devil's Spout.

"See why you need to learn to swim?" says Luke, pointing at an extra high one.

The sky is so dark that the seagulls show up really well – ragged and white, tossed in the wind.

"I just wish this rain would stop," I grumble. I'm desperate to get up to Gull Head.

"I don't think we should go digging today, even if it does get sunny," says Luke. "All the adults are watching us."

He does have a point.

"Let's lie low for a bit. In case they start to wonder about the tools."

I sit up straight. "One day, that's all," I tell him. I grab hold of his arm. "Promise me you'll come tomorrow."

I see Luke's eyes get wide and blue, then crinkle at the corners. "OK. OK." He gives me a great big smile. "Keep your hair on. I'm only teasing. I know how you're so impatient."

"I'm not impatient. We *have* to be in a hurry," I say. "It's serious."

"Yeah, I know." He pushes his hair back out of his eyes. His face and neck are very brown and the bead on its leather round his neck looks like it's part of him. "I'm going out with the boys tonight – if it stops raining. D'you wanna come?"

I feel a sort of warm flicker inside.

"But it might be a good idea if you stayed in. To cover for me." He gives me his quick cat-smile.

"All right," I say. "But I'm coming next time."

"Sure."

I get into bed thinking about me and Luke digging up the gold together. I can just see the looks on Mum's and Rosa's faces when we come staggering in with pockets full of coins.

I lie in the dark and close my eyes. The rain has stopped at last. All I can hear is the waves moving in and out, in and out, rushing and rolling up the beach.

There's thumping and doors banging. Someone's shouting and the lights go on in the hall.

What's going on? I jump out of bed and run downstairs. The kitchen door's wide open. Rosa and Jim and a man I've never seen before are in the middle of the room. Rosa has tears streaming down her face, Jim is holding out his arms and Rosa is fighting him off with both hands.

"Calm down, love. Go and get dressed, Albert'll wait a minute. Go and get some proper clothes; it'll be cold on the boat."

"No! No!" Rosa shouts, struggling away, and she's trying to pull on her wellies, but she still has her pyjamas on.

The old man, Albert, is just standing there.

Something awful's happened. There's a buzzing in my head like it's about to explode.

Luke, something's happened to Luke.

Jim sees me in the doorway. "Run upstairs and get Rosa's fleece and her jeans, Effie."

For a minute I can't move. Then I run, up the stairs and into Rosa and Jim's bedroom. I go in quietly, careful not to wake Bee. She's in her cot under the window, lying on her back with her arms in Vs, like wings. Her hands are curled into two little balls each side of her head.

I grab the clothes from the chair in the corner and race back downstairs.

Mum's in the kitchen too, now, and she takes the clothes from me. Jim and Mum help Rosa into her jeans and fleece over the top of her pyjamas. It's like dressing a doll, or like Rosa is a baby.

I'm shaking. I want to know what's happened but I'm scared. I'm too scared to ask.

Albert comes over. "The boy's had a fall," he says, softly. "He's in a bad way. I'm taking his mum over in the boat to the hospital."

"I'm coming too!" I run to get my fleece from the pile in the corner.

"No," says Jim. "You stay here, Effie."

I look at Rosa. Her eyes are big and dark with lines of tears down her white, white face.

"Stay and help your mum with Bee," she tells me.

Jim opens the door and they go out with Albert into the black night.

The room seems empty with just Mum and me.

"Will he be all right?" I ask.

"I hope so. They've taken him to the hospital on the mainland, so it's serious." She says it like she's thinking out loud.

"I'm frightened," I tell her.

"So am I."

Then Bee starts up, a high, thin wail. Mum goes to her and I get her milk. By the time I get upstairs, she's roaring her head off.

Mum's walking round the room, jiggling Bee in her arms. I show Mum where the clean nappies are and together we put a new one on.

We go into Mum's bed, all three of us, and snuggle down. The sun's just coming up at the edge of the sea, and the night's turning to morning. Bee takes her bottle with big greedy sucks. Little trails of milk bubble out the sides of her mouth and trickle down her chin. She finishes and closes her eyes, and I put the empty bottle on the floor.

Mum is lying still but she's not asleep; she's just staring out the window at the empty sky, with the saddest face in the world.

I close my eyes. I see Crow House with no lights on, the front door swinging open and closed, open and closed. In my dream, a white 'For Sale' sign creaks and groans in the wind.

All next morning we don't hear anything from the hospital. We keep checking the mobile in case there's a text. There's not much food for breakfast. Mum hasn't collected her pay from the Anchor, so there's hardly any money either.

"Maybe we'll go to the shop later," she says. "Bee needs to go out, I suppose."

Mum looks terrible. Her face is white and she's got these purple marks under her eyes. She's started biting her nails again.

Bee is quiet for once, sitting in her highchair sucking on a breadstick.

I hear tapping at the back door. I open it and

old Mrs Bowton from the corner shop is here with two carrier bags. "We've put together a bit of a present," she says. She comes in and lifts the bags on the table. "There's some milk and bread and a bit of cheese. Oh, and some juice for the baby."

"Thank you," says Mum, half-standing up, while I dive in to see if there are any biscuits. There are, with chocolate on too.

"Terrible business," says Mrs Bowton, standing in the middle of the kitchen with her hands in her pockets. "I don't suppose there's any news, is there?"

Mum shakes her head and sinks back down in the chair again.

"Well, I'll be going then." Mrs Bowton smiles at me. "Here you are, dear. I don't know your name, Little Redhead. You look just like your granny when she was young, you do."

She pulls two coins out of her jacket pocket and presses them into my hand. "One for the boy," she whispers, "let's hope he …"

I nod.

All morning we get visitors. Everyone brings bags of food, cakes, sweets and fruit. Mum's boss from the Anchor comes with her pay and gives me five pounds too. Everyone asks for news of Luke. And we haven't any. And they go away. I stuff myself with biscuits and cake and crisps. None of it makes me happy. I just keep thinking about Luke.

I try to play with Bee but she's whiny. At lunchtime, I put her in her highchair and feed her one of Rosa's special baby meals from the fridge. I warm it carefully first, and make sure I stir it properly, just like Rosa showed me.

Bee just frowns and spits it out. "Wosa, Wosa," she says, over and over again.

"I can't stand all this waiting," says Mum, checking her phone for the millionth time. She opens a bottle of wine and takes it into the front room to watch telly.

Next thing, she's back in the kitchen with the mobile in her hand.

"Jim's sent a text. Not good news," she says. "They're going to operate."

That buzzing is back in my head again and I don't hear what else she says.

"Wosa, Wosa," Bee's keeping on.

"He won't die, will he?" It comes out as a whisper.

"I don't think so," says Mum.

The day drags by. Jim's staying with Rosa while they do the operation on Luke, sometime later. He broke some ribs and his arm in two places, falling onto rocks. But they think he's bleeding inside too, and that's the most dangerous thing.

That's all we know.

It's really sunny and hot out. I think about how Luke and me should be digging up the treasure. Instead, he's in hospital and I might never see him again. I feel cold and sick.

I put Bee in her cot for a nap but she won't sleep. I bring her back to the kitchen and build towers for her with bricks. She knocks them down with her fat little hands. I have to keep watching her. She crawls over to Shadow and pushes her face right into the kitten-box. I'm scared she'll get scratched.

I'm scared of everything.

Mum's supposed to be working tonight. She calls in sick, just like the old days. I don't want her to lose her job.

"It's OK, Fee," she tells me. "They all know about Luke, down at the Anchor. They won't expect me to leave you and Bee on your own."

Twenty-five

It's nearly teatime when the doorbell goes. No one ever rings the doorbell.

Mum dashes through the house to open the front door, and I'm right behind her with Bee struggling in my arms. My heart is thumping and a voice in my head keeps saying, "Please make Luke be OK. Please make him be OK."

Raine nearly falls through the door. "Oh, thank goodness – they told me a child was in hospital – I thought – Effie!" And she throws her arms right round Mum. "Thank goodness she's safe!"

Raine says it over and over, and Mum sort of

folds up and Raine's hugging her. Then her head goes down into Mum's hair and Mum's hugging her back, and huge sobs are coming from both of them. Bee starts moaning and wriggling, so Raine pulls me to her and everyone's crying at once.

Raine's face is covered with tears and she won't let go of me or Mum. "I was on the ferry. They told me it was a child, a child from Crow House. Thank goodness they were wrong."

"They weren't wrong: it's Luke. He fell." Mum tells Raine about Luke, and about how bad he is.

"I can't imagine how Rosa is feeling," Mum says. "She was in a terrible state last night."

By now Bee is yelling her head off. We all go into the kitchen and Mum puts the kettle on for another bottle for Bee.

As I sit at the table with Bee on my lap, giving her the milk, Mum and Raine talk and talk, and they're *holding hands*. But they're not talking about Luke and Rosa any more, they're back in the past.

"I'm so sorry, Penny," Raine says, "I must have been a horrible mother to you. But I was just trying to keep you safe. That's what all the rules were for; to protect you."

"And I must have been a horrible child, doing everything you told me not to. A wild child." Mum is laughing and crying at the same time.

"All those wasted years. I'm so glad you've come home," says Raine.

"I am too," Mum tells her. "And I know Effie is as well, even though she didn't want to come. That right, Effie?"

I nod my head like mad.

"Does that mean we can stay at Crow House?"

"I can't promise that, Effie," Raine says gently. "But I promise we'll find you all another place to live – somewhere a bit more modern."

It's late when Raine leaves and it's very late when the mobile rings. We're in Mum's bed, like last night, because Bee won't settle down.

Mum answers "Yes" and "No" and I have to squeeze right up close to hear Jim talking. All he says is they've done the operation and Rosa's waiting to see the doctor. There's no more news. Mum tells him that Bee is fine, which is mainly true. She clicks the phone shut and sighs. I feel her start to cry again, her whole body shaking and rocking next to me in the darkness.

"Poor, poor Rosa," she says.

And I'm crying again too, pressing myself against her, thinking of Luke smiling his quick cat-smile.

Mum's phone rings again in the middle of the night. She listens for ages and ages and I lie next to her, stiff and straight and scared. "Please make him be OK," goes the voice inside my head, again and again and again.

Mum switches off. "Effie?" she asks. "Are you awake?"

I nod but I can't make any words come out.

"It's not good," Mum says in a whisper.

Bee wriggles between us, hot under the covers.

I wait, holding my breath.

"They want us to go over in the morning. To take Bee to see him. Just in case …"

And then I tell her. How I knew Luke was going out, I knew he was going free-running and I didn't tell anyone this time. "If I'd told Rosa she would've stopped him. But I just let him go."

I'm sobbing now and Mum's holding me and stroking my hair.

"Shh," she says. "It's not your fault. Luke's a free-runner, it's part of him. Rosa knows that; you can't protect someone all the time. He was unlucky last night. Must've been all that rain, made the rocks slippery."

I fall asleep with Mum stroking my hair.

The next morning is a blur. Somehow we give Bee her breakfast and put some clean clothes in a bag for Rosa and Jim, and some spare clothes for us. I remember the nappies and a bottle for Bee. I run upstairs to my room and pull out the treasures hidden under my bed. I slide them inside my pillowcase, under my pillow, and fluff the duvet on top.

I wonder if there's anything I should take for Luke? I run into his room and stand staring round at all his things. I look at the pinboard next to his bed and see a photo of him and his mates, up on Higher Rock. His head is back and he's laughing. Carefully I take it down and slip it into my pocket.

When we get right down to the quay, it's busy and loud. The big white ship's already in with a queue of people shuffling on board. We stand at the end of the line and wait. Bee starts grumbling, wriggling about in the buggy 'til it rocks.

Suddenly, there's a shout: "PENNY! EFFIE!" Someone comes hurtling along the quay. It's Raine with her jacket open and her hair flying out behind her in the wind. She runs up to us but the ferry man comes along and tells us we'd better hurry. He helps with the buggy and Mum, Bee and me go up the ramp to find some seats.

Mum calls out to Raine, "Thanks for coming!"

Raine gives a little wave. "If there's anything I can do …?"

I remember Shadow and the kittens. I lean over the rail and yell, "There's no one to feed the cats!"

"I'll go over twice a day!" Raine calls back.

It's a long ride on the ferry. I feel sick again, so we sit on the deck. Bee cries and cries until her face is all red blotches, wet with tears and snot. I'm too tired to play with her so Mum walks up and down with Bee in her arms, singing old songs.

When we get to the mainland, Jim meets us. He kisses me and his face is rough and prickly where he hasn't shaved. Bee squeals when she sees him; he hugs her to him 'til she squeaks. All the way to the bus stop we sing 'The Wheels on the Bus' until we've done all the verses we can think of. But I'm only making myself sing. Inside, I'm sad and quiet.

The hospital is a long, grey building with orange roses in front. A smiley nurse takes us to where Rosa and Luke are.

At a big glass door she stops. The sign says Intensive Care. We have to squirt freezing cold liquid on our hands from a box on the wall, to kill the germs. Suddenly, I don't want to go in. Jim and Bee and Mum walk through but my legs just stop moving.

I shove my hand in the pocket of my jeans, turning the golden coin over and over, making a wish.

The nurse comes back for me. "There are lots

of tubes and things and some noisy machines, but he's the same boy underneath," she tells me. "He can't talk to you, though I think he can hear you."

I want to ask her loads of questions but I don't. She pushes open the door for me and I go inside.

Luke is in a white bed with machines all round him. His broken arm is wrapped in a massive white bandage. He's lying straight and still. A tube is coming out of his mouth and his face is grey. The machines make gurgling, sighing noises, in and out, Darth Vader noises. I know it's the sound of Luke breathing. Or maybe it's the machines doing the breathing, keeping him alive. His eyes are closed.

Rosa is next to him with Bee on her lap. She's holding Luke's hand, and there's a tube trailing from it. Rosa looks like all the colour has gone out of her. She doesn't even see me; her eyes are on Luke's face.

My legs are shaking so hard I think I'll fall over. The Darth Vader noises go *sigh, gurgle, sigh, gurgle*.

This is the worst day of my life.

Twenty-six

We stay on the mainland at Jim's friend's place. The house stinks of curry because there's a takeaway next door. Mum and me squeeze into one small bed and listen to the people laughing in the street outside. Car doors slam. A police car whizzes by *nee, nah, nee, nah.*

I squinch my eyes shut and think of the sea.

Next day we visit Luke again. I hate the long walk to the bus stop with Mum. I hate the smell of cars on the road and fifty million people crammed into the bus with us. I hate not knowing if Luke will be OK.

I breathe on the bus window until it's all steamed up and write

!IH

on the glass.

When we get to the hospital, Luke's just the same as yesterday. We sit on hard plastic chairs and talk to him, even though he can't answer us. Rosa holds his hand and stares into his face.

"You talk to him, Effie; tell him what you've been doing."

"Remember when we went to Giants' Hall?" I say. "Remember Crow House – and the kittens?"

Luke says nothing.

When he wakes up, will he remember anything at all?

Mum sighs and shuffles about on her chair. "I think we'll go home soon, unless Rosa wants us to stay. We don't seem to be doing any good here," she says quietly.

The next morning, the nurse meets us outside the door to Luke's room.

My stomach twists.

"There's been a little progress," she tells us. "He's not responding as quickly as we'd hoped but there are a few good signs."

I rush in – and it's all exactly the same, except the breathing machine has gone. Rosa is sitting next to Luke and holding his hand. She looks across at me and kind of smiles. And Luke's eyes aren't open.

"You can talk to him, I'm sure he knows what we're saying. He's trying to get better," Rosa says, "he's trying to squeeze my hand."

I push in next to her and she moves back a bit in her chair, letting Luke's hand drop on the bedclothes. I put my hand in his. Nothing happens.

"Here's Effie come to see you," Rosa tells him. "Say hello to her."

There's the tiniest movement. I think there is.

And I jabber away about nothing, about everything. I tell him all about the curry-ish place we're staying in, and about how horrible it is here on the mainland. I talk about my dream of the 'For Sale' sign on Crow House and how Raine and Mum are friends again.

Rosa goes to get a cup of coffee and a doctor comes in to check on Luke.

"He's still a very sick young man," she tells me, "but he's out of danger. He'll have to stay in hospital for a while, so we can keep an eye on him. His arm is very badly broken in several places so he won't be climbing again for some time."

Poor Luke.

We stay 'til the end of visiting time then Mum and me say goodbye; we're catching the ferry home tomorrow.

At the door, I remember the photo.

"I forgot something," I say to Mum.

"Don't be long. I'll wait here for you."

I dodge back in. Luke's eyes are still closed. I rummage around in my rucksack and pull out the photograph of him standing on the rock. I put it on the table next to his bed.

"As soon as I can, I'll get the treasure." I whisper, in case anyone hears. "Tomorrow evening, I'll be up at Gull Head."

Luke's eyelids seem to flutter.

"Don't go … on your own," he says. His voice is ever so quiet, a ghost-voice. But he's real. He's alive.

"I'll be OK," I tell him.

He lifts his arm from the bed. Around his wrist is a hospital bracelet made of paper, with LUCAS MOON in black letters.

Luke is gently nudging my hand with his, trying to push something towards me. It's his sea-bead on its string of leather, brown against the white hospital sheets. "For luck," he whispers.

I take it.

"For luck," I agree, pulling it carefully over my head.

Twenty-seven

There's no rain today. The sun is a huge yellow ball in a blue, blue sky. I stand on deck at the front of the ferry, holding on to the rail, speeding out to sea. Heading home. The salty wind whips my hair against my face and my eyes water. I think about the figureheads in the Giant's Hall – the lady in the blue dress, proud and strong; the fierce tiger.

Luke's sea-bead is safe round my neck, bringing me luck. The golden coin is deep in my pocket.

I just know I'll find the treasure today.

Twenty-eight

We open the back door to the sounds of squeaking kittens. In the kitchen, Shadow stands up in the box to say hello. Her babies wriggle and squirm around her, balls of fur – stripes and spots – with tiny pink feet.

"Look. The little ginger one can get out of the box all on its own."

The kitten tumbles over the edge of the box and staggers about on the kitchen floor, peeping and mewing. Shadow gently lifts it in her mouth and plops it back into bed, safe on the pink cardigan. I stroke each kitten in turn.

"Ahh," goes Mum, kneeling down next to

me on the floor. "Aren't they sweet? I'd love to spend the evening drawing them. I'm exhausted; maybe I should give the Anchor a ring – maybe they don't need me today after all?"

I look up fast, to see if she's joking. "No, you must go to work – or you might lose your job," I say, thinking quickly. "You haven't been in for days."

Mum takes forever to get ready. I sit on her bed watching her get dressed. She puts on some jeans and a white blouse, then pulls it all off again. Next, she's in her long black skirt and a flowery top.

"Argh, nothing looks right," she moans, tearing it off.

My rucksack is waiting in my bedroom, with Bob's trowel at the bottom. Why won't she just hurry up?

Mum leans in close to the mirror, gives her lips a smear of gloss, and frowns. "Mm, must do something with my hair."

In the mirror, her eyes look straight into mine.

She turns round to me, kneeling on the bed on one knee, and reaches over to touch Luke's sea-bead round my neck. She smells of mints and roses body spray.

"Why did he give you this, I wonder?" She stares right into my face.

I feel myself going red.

"I'm taking care of it for him," I mumble, pulling away.

I go to my bedroom, closing the door behind me. I dive onto my bed and feel inside my pillowcase for the torc and the brooch. I bring them out and lay them on my duvet, stroking the carving of the bird's feathers and the dips and dents of the golden rope with the tips of my fingers.

Wait 'til I get the rest up and show it all to Luke.

The door bursts open. Quick as a flash, I stuff the treasure into my rucksack and drop it down by the side of my bed.

Mum pokes her head in. "I've got to go now. I won't be very late, I'm shattered," she says. She opens my door a bit wider. "Raine might call in sometime …"

"Raine?" I say. "Why's she coming here?"

"Just to see how you are."

"MUM?"

The stairs creak, the back door bangs and she's gone.

I belt into Luke's bedroom to get his rucksack – I reckon I'll need two bags – pull on my hoodie and dash down the path.

I'm on my way at last, through the gate and running along the coast path. The torc is weighing me down a bit but it's too late to go back now; Raine might be here any minute.

"Effie!"

It is Raine, bumping up the hill in the Land Rover with her head sticking out of the window, calling me. Can I pretend I haven't seen her?

"Effie! Here a minute!"

I stop. I wriggle the two rucksacks further up my shoulder and trail over to the dusty green van. Raine turns the engine off and steps onto the grass. She's got jeans and a stripy tee shirt on today, and her hair's hanging to her shoulders. She looks a billion years younger than usual.

"Thanks for feeding the cats," I say, polite and calm. Inside, I'm racing along that path to Gull Head.

She smiles. "I enjoyed it, the big cat is such a good mum; very attentive – and she won't stand any nonsense from them, will she? But she's very gentle." She laughs, twisting her keys round and round in one hand.

I laugh a bit too.

"How's Lucas looking today?" she asks. "I've been ringing the hospital, they say there's a slight change."

"He's OK. He can talk again," I tell her.

A gust of wind blows off the sea and lifts Raine's hair in a silver cloud.

I shuffle my feet a bit.

"Where are you going?" she asks. "It's rather late in the day for a walk, isn't it?"

I shake my head hard. Why won't she *go*?

I can see her clever eyes on the rucksacks, trying to work it out. And I nearly tell her; I open my mouth to – but I've promised Luke. I've promised him I'll get the treasure, just like we planned.

"Thanks again, for the cats," I say instead, giving her the biggest smile I can.

I turn back to the cliff path and walk away from Raine, at slow snail's speed.

All the time, I can feel her staring at me and I'm just waiting for her to call out one more time – and if she does, I'll run like crazy, because I bet I'm faster than her.

But she doesn't. I hear the van door slam and the engine start up. The tyres crunch as she turns it round, and the Land Rover purrs away.

Twenty-nine

I carry on along the cliff to Gull Head, through the prickly yellow gorse that smells of coconuts and through the purple heather. You can tell it's been raining; the ground's all squelchy under my trainers, sucking me down. The treasure in my rucksack bumps against my back *thump, thump, thump.*

I get to the digging place and it's just as I left it. I pull the rucksacks off my shoulders and stuff Luke's bag down in the ferns, 'til it's almost hidden. I push my hand into the pocket of my jeans and pull out my golden coin. I tuck it safely into the pocket of my rucksack and zipper it shut; no point losing it while I'm digging. Down on my knees, I squeeze in behind the boulder and dig with my hands, using Bob's trowel when I get down to the difficult stuff. However long it takes, I'm not giving up today.

I'm not going home without the gold.

Further in I go until the gap's big enough for me to slip right in. I dig faster and faster, using the trowel just like Raine showed me, poking it between the rocks, scooping and clearing out the tiny stones and mud. The earth is different this time, softer, with bubbles of grey mud frothing round the stones.

On my knees I wriggle deeper into the passageway, dragging my rucksack with me, pushing forwards. Soon it's getting tight again and I can't breathe properly; it's dark and stinking of mud and those panicky feelings are starting up in my chest – but I make myself carry on slowly, bit by bit. I must be nearly at the place where I got blocked last time.

Suddenly everything's moving – the ground under my knees, the earth on top of me. I stick out my hands to stop myself. I can't. The tunnel falls in and I'm falling too. Everything's tumbling down, down – soil and stones, roots and mud.

My rucksack's torn from my hand.

Earth's in my mouth, I'm spitting and coughing, grabbing at rocks, at anything, but it's all moving together. I'm screaming and coughing and breathing soil.

I bang to a stop.

I can't move my legs. My breath comes in sharp pants. It hurts. Everything hurts so much.

I'm lying on my front with my face pressed against stone. It's dark but just light enough to make out the shapes of the rocks in the walls, my arms out in front of me. Stones pitter-pitter and loose earth falls. The sea rolls and crashes nearby. Everything's holding me down – rocks and piles of earth. I wriggle and twist. There's a heavy pile of stuff on my back.

I'm trapped.

More earth shifts and falls, I can hear it scooting away, down and down. Echoing. There must be another tunnel there, next to me, something I can't see.

My heart is thumping so loud I can hear it.

What if I'm stuck here for ever? What's going to happen to me? What if I never see Mum or anyone ever again?

I cry, proper big tears, hot on my face, and

snot comes down my nose. I stretch forward to wipe my face on my arm but I can't stop crying.

I should've listened to Luke. I should've told Jim or Raine. My mouth is full of grit and earth. I'm going to die in this tunnel and no one knows where I am.

What would Luke do now?

He wouldn't think too much, he'd just get on with it.

I twist again and pull my leg up as hard as I can. The earth and rocks shake all around me. I pull and tug, over and over again.

I panic. I roll about, side to side, trying to get the heavy stuff off. One leg is nearly free. I kick and kick. My leg shoots out to the side, and a heap of stones and soil goes crashing away.

Now I wriggle the other foot, kicking and twisting like a mad thing. I push on the ground with my arms and my free leg – the soil and stones shift and break and fall.

I'm free.

I roll over onto my side.

I'm in a small cave, with a low roof of stones above me. My heart is hammering loud. How will I get out?

Boom, crash-ssh, Boom, crash-ssh go the waves.

I take great gulps of air but I can't breathe properly. I pant and gulp, pant and gulp. All I can taste is earth. My body aches. Tears keep sliding out of my eyes and I don't stop them.

Then I see it.

I'm face to face with a skeleton. Its round, black eyeholes stare right at me, its mouth is open, grinning wide.

As my eyes get used to the blackness, I see more bones – another tiny skeleton, curled up by its side, turned towards me in the dark.

I scramble to get away from them, scratching and scrabbling as fast as I can.

I'm buried alive.

The panic comes again and I can't breathe. I pant and pant. The air is thick and wet, and I can't fill up my lungs. How can I get out? What can I do?

"Keep moving." That's what Luke would say.

Above me, far away, is a slit of light – the sky.

Trying not to look at the skeletons, I shuffle on my knees across earth and stones, towards the light. Every movement makes the rock shift and crumble.

Suddenly the ground runs out; my knees are on the edge of nothingness. I wriggle backwards.

I'm on a kind of ledge. The tunnel goes upwards, the way I fell in, and downwards too. Below me, there's grey rocks and the sand of a beach, and the foamy white tips of waves.

Hell's Mouth, Luke called it.

Way below me, on the rocks, I can just make out the shape of my rucksack. I watch the waves crawl up the rocks – *hissss* – long silver tongues of waves, lapping and licking at the bag, then – *ahhhh* – sinking away again. My heart is thumping. Not my treasure. No! The waves reach higher – the bag moves – there's nothing I can do. I watch until my eyes sting – and the sea covers my bag completely, carrying it off with the brooch and the torc and my little golden coin inside.

A massive sob bursts out of me. My treasure is gone. I've been robbed; the sea's stolen it all.

But I'm still alive.

Very carefully, I put one foot into the tunnel and test it. Will it hold my weight? Slowly, slowly I begin to crawl upwards. One leg, then an arm, and push. Then the other leg, the other arm. Push. I grab at the rocks with my hands like an animal, clawing my way. Bit by bit, I scramble upwards, with loose earth and stones falling all around me. The slit of sky slowly gets bigger and bigger – I can smell the cold, fresh air.

I'm shuddering, my fingers are numb. I grab a rock and it crumbles away. My whole body jolts and slips; I'm clawing and snatching – at nothing.

I fall. Down I go again, right down, rocks and soil and dirt like heavy black rain. I stick out my hands, grabbing and clutching – but everything's torn away from me, faster and faster, everything's on the move. Again.

Bang.

I stop. My whole body is stuck, hanging in the tunnel.

I move my head – just the tiniest bit – and see the light above me, still there but much further away now. The rocks around me wobble. My arms are so tired. I try to heave myself upwards, to start the journey again – but I've got no strength left.

It's so unfair. I was nearly there. I was almost out – but I just can't do it. And no one knows I'm here.

The waves thunder on the rocks.

I remember – the sea's coming in.

Thirty

The waves are coming in fast now, I can hear them sloshing about below me, with a deep, cold echo. My chest hurts and I've no breath left. I shut my eyes. I see Rosa running across the green field in her flowery dress. Luke, standing on the sea wall, with the sea-bead round his neck. I see the blue sky and the crashing white waves, and Mum's face. I hear her singing, like she's singing me to sleep:

"*I saw the new moon dah-dah-dah ...*"

My eyes flicker open and it's much darker; the slit of light above me shows the purple night sky. My whole body hurts and I'm freezing cold. *Shh-ah, Shh-ah* go the waves. I bite my lip, trying to stop my teeth from chattering. I press my face into the rock and bits crumble away and – *plop!*

There's sea just below me, filling up the tunnel.

I'm going to drown.

I let my eyes close and I hang, shivering, in the dark.

And the sea gets me. It grabs my trainers with one ice-cold rush, sending an ache of pain up through my legs. My arms are useless and heavy, wedged against rock. Water rises up to my waist, faster now, dragging me, tugging me down with a giant's pull. I can smell it, fierce and dark and salty. My whole body is shaking with cold. Up to my chest the freezing water comes, pulling and hauling, much, much stronger than me. I squeeze my eyes tight shut.

In the cave, the skeleton's mouth is grinning wide. Round its neck is a circle of gold. There's gold bracelets, too – two round each of its arms, and, nearby, a pot of golden coins, twinkling in the blackness.

The treasure. A grave full of treasure.

Ever so slowly, I push myself forward on my knees, closer to the skeleton. I reach out one hand and touch a bracelet. The metal falls – clang – and the whole bone falls to the ground.

There's more clanging. Louder. I open my eyes. The sky above me is dark now; the slit of purple night has gone.

I hear men shouting, "Effie! Effie!"

Is it real – or a dream?

And Mum's voice, screaming, "Effie! Are you there?"

There's bright lights shining into the cave.

I'm shouting and crying both at the same time, "Yes! Help! HELP!" And I try to wave but my arms won't work. I'm shivering and shaking and my teeth are chattering.

"I'm here!" I shout. It's only a tiny shout; they won't hear me.

The lights flicker away.

"HELP!" I try again.

The lights come back and there's faces looking down. "OK. We've got you!" shout the men.

My heart leaps.

I wait and I wait, keeping my eyes fixed on the little round beams of light. There's banging and scraping from above – and the hole gets bigger. I see a man climb in; slowly, slowly, he comes crawling down to me, digging out the rocks with a kind of metal bar, passing the stones up to the men behind him. He's got a torch fixed on his head, flashing on the rocks – shadow and light – all around. Nearer and nearer he comes but so slowly.

It's a long, long time and my eyes keep closing. All I want to do is sleep but Mum's shouting to me – I can see her face at the hole: "Don't go to sleep, Fee! Let's sing. What shall we sing, Fee? 'She'll be Coming Round the Mountain When She Comes'?"

Mum starts up with that old baby song, and I can hear the crying in her voice.

I'm so tired. But I do try to sing, for Mum. It comes out in a croak.

We sing it together, Mum and me.

Thirty-one

I can breathe the fresh, clean air. I can see the moon. And at last I'm in Mum's arms. I push my face in her hair to smell the mints and roses and she hugs me tight.

"HOORAY!" A great cheer goes up as they carry me to the ambulance. Looks like the whole island is here at Gull Head. Raine's here, and Mum's boss from the Anchor, and Mr and Mrs Bowton from the corner shop. Even the man from the chippie.

I try to lift my arm, to give them all a wave. I don't manage that – but I do a thumbs up instead.

FLASH! goes a camera.

Thirty-two

I'm in the same hospital as Luke.

Mum and Rosa and Jim and Bee are squeezed round my bed. There's a nurse called Fiona, too, who's really nice. Luke is next to me with his sea-bead back round his neck and a big purple bandage on his arm. You can even whack it and it doesn't hurt, only we're not meant to do that.

Raine's here, with a massive basket of fruit: grapes and plums and nectarines. Thanks, Raine. She puts it down on the table next to my bed and picks up a newspaper from the pile. I'm in all the newspapers. 'YOUNG TREASURE SEEKER RISKS LIFE – AND FINDS TOMB!' it says in the best one, with the photo of me giving the thumbs up sign.

Raine smiles. "It's not the way I would have done it – but you've made a major discovery, Effie. The island is very much back on the map; we're going to move our dig up to Gull Head."

"But there's no treasure."

I've told them about the brooch, the coin and the golden torc, all carried off by the waves.

"Not treasure as you mean it." Raine gives that laugh of hers. "I had a look in your cave – and I'm pretty sure it's an Iron Age burial."

"Bones and old pottery – that's all," I say, just to tease her.

Raine sits down on the bed and waves the newspaper at me. She's smiling a big, proper smile. "It's treasure to me – enough to allow me to stay on the island and begin some new work."

Luke nudges me with his good arm. "Ask about Crow House. Go on!"

He knows something I don't.

"I won't have to sell the house now, Effie. You can all stay – as long as you like," Raine says.

Everyone's laughing and saying, "Well done, Effie," and Bee's clapping her hands together like crazy.

I've done it! I've saved Crow House – and we can all stay together.

I feel like a millionaire.

At six o'clock Fiona hands me the remote.

"Shh, everyone." I flick on the TV.

There I am, up on Gull Head, being lifted out of the tunnel. The reporter says about all the skeletons and the secret cave above Hell's Mouth, how Mum came searching for me and how Raine knew which way I'd gone – and about my incredible rescue.

Then they're on to the weather.

I've been on telly.

How amazing is that!

Thirty-three

It's Luke's first evening home.

Rosa's got a fish stew in the oven with baked potatoes and everything. While it's cooking, we all sit in the front room. Raine's brought a book of old photographs with her, of Mum and Jim when they were little kids, mucking about in the sand.

"Look at this one," says Raine, pointing to a blurry picture of a boy and girl holding up a giant crab. "Remember how you cried when we put it back in the sea?"

"Yeah, we called it Samson," says Jim.

Mum screws up her face. "I remember that. Didn't it stink?"

Luke, Bee, Rosa and me are down on the floor, playing with the kittens and a pink rubber mouse. Luke bounces it hard off the floor and the kittens spring after it.

"They're huge now," says Luke, "and really fast."

"Yes, and they have huge appetites too," Rosa tells him. "We can't keep them all –"

"But we *are* keeping Boo," I tell him, pointing to the ginger one. I've named her Boudicca after that fierce old queen we did in History – Boo for short.

Rich fishy smells waft through from the kitchen, making my stomach growl. It's getting late and the sun's going down. Suddenly the whole room is flooded with golden light.

"When's tea?" Luke asks, catching Boo with both hands and plopping her down in Rosa's lap.

"Half an hour," Rosa says, "so don't go disappearing, you two."

Luke and me grin across at each other.

"Just time to go down to the beach – and back again," Luke says.

"Take care of that arm!" Rosa shouts as we slip through the kitchen and out the back door.

We don't run down the hill, in case Luke falls

over or something, but we're still pretty fast. By the time we're at the beach, I'm puffing.

The waves come booming in, spraying us with milky white foam.

Luke and me muck about on the sand, wobbling on rocks, slipping on shiny seaweed.

"Dare you to get your feet wet!" Luke shouts above the row.

"No way!" I scream back.

Soon I've had enough. I stand at the top of the beach while Luke dodges around at the sea's edge, getting soaked.

I stare at the moving waves. I think of how they crawled onto the rocks and stole my treasure, filling up the sea cave, dark and deep and cold.

I shudder.

For the zillionth time, I wonder where my brooch and torc are now.

Luke runs up next to me. "Better go." I can just work out what he's saying over the noise.

We turn away from the beach and walk back towards the hill. The sun is sinking slowly down into the sea, spreading gold right across the bay.

"Do you think the waves will bring it back?" I ask him.

He knows I'm talking about my treasure.

"No, you'll have to go in and get it," he tells me. "As soon as this plaster comes off, I'll teach you to swim. When you're good enough, we can go diving – off the side of Albert's boat. I bet he'll let us."

Swimming *and* diving.

"Maybe," I say.

I think of my brooch and torc, lying deep, deep down on the sea bottom.

Maybe I *will* go and get them back one day.

Two figures come across the beach towards us: Mum in front with her hair blowing out, silvery gold, and Raine behind.

"Rosa's sent us to herd you home!" Raine calls.

"It's starting to get dark early," Mum says. "Take care you don't slip on the rocks."

I look down – and here it is in front of me, peeping out of the sand: a sea-bead, conker-brown. A sea-bead of my own. I kneel down and pick it out of its sandy bed. I balance it, round and fat, in my open hand for everyone to see.

Luke and Mum and Raine crowd in.

"I knew you'd find one soon," Luke says.

Raine bends her head to have a closer look.

"Yes, she's a proper islander now."

I'm grinning away like anything.

Mum touches the bead with one finger and rolls it about. "That's your real treasure," she says quietly.

I close my hand over the bead and push it down into the pocket of my jeans, safe and sound 'til we get home. And I know I'll put it on a string of leather to wear round my neck, like everyone else in my family.

A NOTE FROM THE AUTHOR

Archaeology is a real life history puzzle. Putting the pieces together, recording what we find and sharing our knowledge helps build a picture of the past and how people lived. And we can pass all this information on for people in the future.

Effie makes an archaeological discovery – but she's not a good archaeologist. Digging for treasure as she does, without training, can damage precious objects and ruin ancient sites. And the site is as important as the find. If soil layers get disturbed, pieces of the puzzle are muddled and confused, and information can be lost for ever. Luke is right: call in the experts. If you ever find an object that you think is ancient, contact your local museum.

Digging's fun and there are plenty of digs you can go on as a volunteer. Trained archaeologists will show you how to excavate properly and help you understand the importance of the things you find.

It's a very special feeling to uncover something like a brooch or a coin that may have fallen from someone's hand thousands of years ago. And it's an even better feeling to shout, "Find!" and know you're sharing it with others. I think so, anyway.

Perhaps I'll see you there.

LINKS

Archeoscan. Digging opportunities for families
and schools in south-west England
enquiries@archeoscan.com
www.archeoscan.com

Young Archaeologists' Club. The only UK-wide
club for young people interested in archaeology
http://www.yac-uk.org/about

Come and visit me on my website
http://www.janineamos.com

ACKNOWLEDGEMENTS

Thanks to Julia Green, for her insight, encouragement and pearls of wisdom; to Kay Leitch, Jenny Landor and Kim Donovan, for giving the book the golden touch; and to archaeologist Debbie Brookes, for her nuggets of advice.

Thank you to the staff at The Boat House in Laugharne, for keeping me going with tea and Welsh cakes;

And to my family – solid gold –

Thanks, Mum and Dad, for the songs, the laughter and the poetry; to Mick, for his endless patience and support; and to Aron, the jewel in the crown and Consultant Extraordinaire.

CPSIA information can be obtained at www.ICGtesting.com
Printed in the USA
LVOW11s1655250914

405879LV00006B/773/P